ENCHANTED TWIST

ENCHANTED TWIST

SCIONS OF MAGIC™ BOOK SEVEN

TR CAMERON   MICHAEL ANDERLE   MARTHA CARR

THE ENCHANTED TWIST TEAM

Thanks to the JIT Readers

Diane L. Smith
Jeff Eaton
Jeff Goode
Dave Hicks
Dorothy Lloyd
Larry Omans
Deb Mader

If I've missed anyone, please let me know!

Editor
Skyhunter Editing Team

DEDICATION

For those who seek wonder around every corner and in each turning page. And, as always, for Dylan and Laurel.

— *TR Cameron*

"I don't know, buddy, this place seriously gives me the creeps." Caliste Leblanc, matriarch of the noble house that bore her surname, peered through the rusty door into the mausoleum ship and grimaced. "Isn't there a good reason for burial at sea? Why store the bodies here?"

Fyre snorted and the scales that covered his canine-sized dragon lizard body shimmered turquoise and scarlet. "The nobles are weird in all kinds of ways. This shouldn't come as a surprise."

They had traversed several clear tubes that stretched from the dock area of the domed city of New Atlantis to their current position at the entrance to one of the wrecks that surrounded the central sphere. The Bermuda Triangle was known to swallow ships, planes, and whatever else braved its borders, and many of those lost conveyances eventually became part of the expanding web of the city. In this case, House Rivette—whose scion now sat on the throne as Empress—had claimed a small military boat as the unlikely cairn for their ancestors' remains.

Their walk had been nerve-wracking as the ship and the cylinder that led to it floated over a large chasm and the remaining buoyancy of the vessel was apparently all that prevented it from falling further and taking the connection to the city with it. The path had swayed and creaked with every step.

The interior of the ship was dimly lit with what looked like flickering tongues of magical flame confined in jars. These provided only enough illumination to see a short distance ahead. Their path had ended at a locked bulkhead door and she had released it with a spell and a command word Emalia had discovered. Her great-aunt, unsurprisingly, had turned out to be a fantastic researcher.

She's fantastic at everything. Showoff. Cali grinned at the memory of the older woman running through the halls of the Leblanc mansion shouting, "I've found the pommel! I've found the pommel!"

Three pieces of the heirloom sword she needed to free her brother still lay beyond her grasp. *Soon to be two,* she reminded herself. And the Draksa's earlier observation was correct. There was nothing normal about the New Atlantean nobles. "You're not kidding."

He turned a wry grin on her. "Except for Wymarc, right?"

Cali rolled her eyes at the mention of the patriarch of House Jehenel, who had been her frequent companion during her visits to New Atlantis. "Shut it, you." She sighed, peered ahead to try to discern what awaited them, and muttered, "It's unfortunate that Emalia couldn't find more information on where in this blasted ship the pommel is." It was merely noise to occupy her brain, not a real complaint. She switched to mental communication with her partner.

"Okay, let's be quiet from here on out."

"Will do." Their two-way telepathy was a recent development in their deepening relationship that made her very happy. While she'd always been able to sense his emotions, talking directly to him was proving far more useful.

"Let's move ahead. Keep your eyes and ears open." She allowed her magic to escape the confines of her skin and stretch without specific intention. In the past, she'd detected secrets that way and she hoped it would lead her to the object she sought.

And once the sword is complete, I'll beat the information I need to save Atreo out of Styrris Malniet with my bare hands if necessary.

She stepped over the bottom lip of the bulkhead and entered the room. The chamber seemed like the kind of place where you'd receive visitors, with space to move to both sides and another door on the opposite wall. The floor was comprised of metal grates, slightly rusted but better preserved than one would expect. Her heavy boots stirred puffs of dust with each step.

She'd chosen to wear her combat clothes, although they'd been hidden under a windbreaker she'd abandoned in the tunnel on the way in. The dark padded jacket with the compass that was her family sigil hung over black pants and a broad belt secured it at her waist. Her light and shield charms hung from a slim silver chain around her neck, and the thick bracelets that would transform into her fighting sticks were snug on her forearms. Healing and energy potions rested in each of her thigh pockets. She was confident that she was ready for whatever lay on the other side of the closed bulkhead across from her.

The wheel protested loudly as she wrenched it in a circle. When the passage finally opened, her assumption was proven wrong. She was decidedly not ready for the abundance of memorials—pictures on the metal walls, somber candles all around that flickered without heat, and handwritten notes stuck to all the vertical surfaces and the shelf that ran at waist level along the perimeter of the room. She used words instead of telepathy, forgetting herself in the moment. "Holy hell."

Speech seemed somehow offensive in the quiet space. She approached a picture at random of a severe-looking woman with upswept grey hair, a sharp, thin face, and eyes that expressed disappointment with the viewer. Beneath it perched a poem full of remembrance, rendered in a child's hand and signed *Shenni*.

Cali shook her head in wonder and returned to mental communication. "*The Empress had a heart once. Imagine.*" The thought of the monarch brought her swiftly to reality. "*Okay, so our enemies aren't completely awful. Only ninety-nine percent awful.*"

Fyre snorted a soft laugh and spoke into her mind. "*You are generous.*"

"*Right?*" She crossed to the next door and yanked on the wheel. When it refused to move, she pushed magic into her arms to strengthen them and tried again. A sharp snapping sound indicated the lock shattering and the barrier released. "*Let's keep searching. Somewhere in this old tub is a piece of my family's sword.*"

As the passage opened, the Draksa asked, *"Did Emalia have any clue why it's in the possession of House Rivette?"*

"No." Cali stepped into the space beyond, a long hallway that led to a four-way intersection. *"But it's safe to assume it has something to do with their betrayal of my parents. That's a debt that still needs to be paid."* And taking back what belongs to me is the first step.

The walls to either side remained metal but were painted black like she'd crossed into a different section of the tomb. They absorbed the scant light and made every-thing seem darker. She considered calling a flame ball, but the ominous sense of danger she'd detected in the initial rooms had increased with each step. Her instincts cautioned her to decide that whatever secrecy she could maintain would be worth the effort. She stepped carefully so her boots wouldn't generate undue sound on the metal beneath her. Fyre, as always, moved as silently as if he were floating.

The spokes to either side at the intersection led to short corridors that ended at closed doors with unrecognizable markers on them. *It's probably their house language.* She opened the one on the right. Beyond it lay a single sarcophagus of heavy grey stone cut at sharp angles into the abstract image of a person, with the stylized shark that was the Rivette house symbol engraved above a string of unfamiliar characters. The black-surfaced room was other-wise empty and nothing indicated what member of the family was buried there. For a moment, she thought about shoving the huge lid aside but quelled the impulse. *"Boring."*

Fyre, who had wandered once around the area while she studied it carefully, nodded. *"Definitely."*

Cali sighed. *"I don't want to check every single room but that's what we'll do if we have to. I feel like it's more likely to be deeper within, so how about we walk to the other side and open everything on our way back?"*

His mental voice was noncommittal. *"Sure. It's as good an idea as any."*

The ship appeared to be largely symmetrical, with chambers on either side at regular intervals all marked with the mysterious symbols. She passed them and progressed deeper into the vessel while she pushed away the sensation of being swallowed by an enormous fish. Occasional staircases led upward but were rendered unusable by metal sheets attached at ceiling height. She nodded toward one. "I guess they don't want us to go upstairs."

"Maybe there's no upstairs to go to. This is a shipwreck, after all."

"That's a good point, fang face." Amusement surged from him, and she grinned at the feeling. Ahead, the corridor ended in another heavy door with a wheel on it. The barrier held many letters in the unknown alphabet. *"I wonder what it says?"*

"Probably 'stay out or we'll kill you.' That's my guess."

She laughed, then stifled the sound. *"You suck. Why would there be death threats on a funeral ship?"*

"Zombies?"

"If House Rivette had zombies, they'd doubtless stand guard everywhere. No, I don't think we have to worry about the undead." She strode forward and grasped the wheel, which refused to budge. Even with magical assistance, her strength was insufficient. She stepped back and frowned at it.

Okay, be that way. Cautiously, she let her magic extend toward the door and discovered wards in place. Fortunately, they didn't trigger at the touch of her power and she narrowed her focus on each in turn. Untangling them was a challenge, but she'd practiced on and off with Emalia and her skills were sufficient to undo them.

When she finally removed the last one, she asked, *"Okay, why would there be wards?"*

Fyre grinned. *"Maybe they're hiding something useful behind it? Like a big room full of zombies and a sword handle?"*

Cali shook her head. "Will you let the zombies thing go, please? I'm sure it's something stupid, probably another corridor." Again, opening the door proved her wrong.

Stepping across the threshold was like entering a different place entirely. She felt the tingle of magic but also a difference in air pressure. It reminded her of movies with science experiments that had to be prevented from leaking out. *Negative pressure, that's what it's called.* Everything seemed muffled and even the vague creaks and groans of the metal that had been her constant companion since she set foot on the ship were absent. Neither of those, however, was as shocking as the sight before her.

Where the front had felt cramped and narrow, the entire back portion of the vessel had been gutted to create one large room. Metal tables like coroners used were arranged perpendicular to the angled walls on both sides to create a strange pattern. What rested on the metal surfaces was the most shocking sight and the two intruders gaped in silence as they tried to make sense of it. A uniform-clad human body stretched on each surface and their chests rose and fell in tandem. Each wore a thick collar around their neck and the synchronicity of it was completely disturbing.

Cali approached cautiously. Fyre walked at her side and she unconsciously extended a hand to touch him and draw comfort from his presence. The first form was female with an utterly blank face, closed eyes, and slack features. If not for the breathing, she would have assumed the woman was deceased.

Okay, maybe the zombie theory has some legs. She checked the next and the ones after that, but the dozen figures were all the same.

Also notable was the complete lack of sword parts anywhere in the room. Only the tables and the bodies were stored there.

"Well, damn. I guess we'll have to go back. Do you have any idea what this is all about? And don't say zombies."

Amusement no longer flowed from the Draksa. *"They don't seem right. I'm not sure what's wrong with them but whatever it is, it's something bad."*

"It's not our problem, though. Who knows what the Empress' family is up to? We already knew we couldn't trust them." She turned to retrace her steps toward the entrance when a whisper of sound from behind made her look over her shoulder in surprise.

Where there had been a dozen inert bodies, twelve wide-awake ones now stood and stared at her. Worse, each of them appeared to be personally angry with her for disturbing their rest. A sense of menace radiated from the group. She raced to the door and darted through a step behind Fyre with the horde of furious possible zombies on her heels.

CHAPTER TWO

Cali spun as soon as she crossed the threshold and fired a cone of electricity at the door she'd passed through. The pursuers had clustered into it, which made the situation an easy one for her to deal with. She'd expected to see them flail and scream when they were bathed in lightning, but once again, her expectations proved incorrect.

The jolt did affect them to some degree and the first one through fell—at least for the moment. Those who followed twitched and jerked as they advanced but the impact of the pain, which was always the most unpleasant result of being struck by electrical magic, didn't seem to materialize. She growled her annoyance. "Okay, lightning won't do it," she muttered, spun away, and ran down the corridor.

She flashed past Fyre, who replied, "Let's try ice." His breath weapon exploded behind her and chills rippled down her spine. She looked over her shoulder and saw that the first two pursuers had been frozen in place. In the moment that followed, those behind flowed around them, and those at the rear began to break the ice shrouds away from their companions. The Draksa turned to run with her. She sent a message to his mind. *"Next right."*

He was on her heels as she made the turn. Their adversaries would be forced into an even smaller funnel, which would give the two teammates a better element of control. They hadn't displayed any magic yet, so she was hopeful that fire would scour the threat away. The first one to round the corner received a blast of flame in the face and fell back as he burned. Although he might not have felt the pain, the damage to his muscles kept him down. She readied herself for the next but it didn't come.

"What the hell?" Cali muttered.

Fyre shook his head, his gaze locked on the corridor ahead. "No idea. Maybe they're scared?"

A loud thumping and clanging noise seemed to materialize from everywhere at once. She looked around involuntarily and wondered what was going on, but the echoing sounds had no apparent source. "What the hell?" she repeated.

"You're very good with words today." The Draksa snorted. "I think the ones you're looking for are 'hull' and 'breaking.'"

"So the not-zombies are trying to put holes in the ship. The one they're currently on."

"Either that or they want to attack us from the sides."

"I dislike both those options."

"Agreed."

"Okay. Let's go get them." She sprinted out of the hallway and turned left while her sticks formed in her hand as the material from her bracelets flowed down her arms. One enemy stood in front of her. He had a sheen of ice in his hair and looked all the angrier for having been momentarily immobilized. Her main concern was getting past him to find those who were trying to damage the boat, so she blasted him with a full power surge of force magic from the tips of her weapons. The man catapulted away like he'd been kicked in the chest, knocked one of his comrades over, and cleared the path to the next intersection.

"I'll go left," she yelled and when she did so, another immediately stood in her path. She had no time to summon magic, only enough to thrust her left stick to block his swinging arm and drive the other one into his chest to hurl him back as he tried to bite her. He caught his balance and attacked again to prevent her from gaining enough distance to cast.

Fine, you want to do it the fun way? Let's dance. She snapped her right stick at his head and when he raised his arm to block, she spun and lashed her left stick backhanded into his ribs. They broke with a resounding crack.

Where a normal assailant would have been at least slowed by the damage, he seemed to not care. He swung his fists at her skull and she deflected one but not the other. The impact blurred her vision and made her ears ring. With an outraged snarl, she dropped her right stick, launched a punch, and wrapped her fist in force magic as it arced toward him. The blow broke his jaw, and the kick she followed it with careened him into the crypt at the end of the hallway. It looked exactly like the one she'd seen earlier, except for the beings that now pounded on the bulkhead with shards of stone they'd apparently broken off the sarcophagus.

Cali filled the room with fire. To her surprise, the figures neither fled nor ran but continued their attempts to savage the hull as if they could break through in time to save themselves. They continued their assault upon the unyielding metal until they fell one by one. Nothing had flowed over her mental channel with Fyre to alarm her subconscious so she was sure he was okay but went to check anyway. The Draksa stood in the center of another burial chamber with bodies frozen in place around him. Those, too, had been dealt with while they attempted to breach the walls.

She tried to recall the original numbers and how many they had incapacitated when a voice issued from the main corridor. "Thieves. Trespassers. How dare you?" She spun as one of the uniformed women stepped into the intersection, her expression haughty above folded arms and a wide-legged stance. "Oh, it's you. The Leblanc girl. Of course it is."

Cali squeezed her sticks, ready for what might come next. When the pause stretched into a longer silence, she decided the woman was waiting for a response. "Matriarch Leblanc to you, whoever or whatever you are."

The laugh uttered by the other woman seemed somehow reluctant.

"*She's like a puppet,*" Fyre sent. "*Not quite in sync.*" Cali nodded. *That's exactly what she's like. Maybe those collars are some kind of control device and the person I'm talking to is hidden around here somewhere?*

Her thoughts were interrupted when the figure shook

her head. "For the moment. Until the noble House Leblanc falls and is swallowed by time, never to be heard from or thought of again."

"Over my dead body." Internally, she groaned. *Great one, Cali. Smooth. Way to set her up.*

The other woman grinned. "What an excellent plan. Goodbye, Matriarch." She turned and sprinted toward the back of the boat. Shortly thereafter, the sound of metal slamming echoed all around her, followed by the gush of water.

"That's not good. Let's find the pommel and get the hell out of here." They managed to clear the first room before the liquid began to seep in above the level of the grate at their feet.

Fyre snorted. "As if water could harm us."

Cali wrenched the door to the next crypt open. "It could if the ship falls and we're trapped. Well, maybe not you, but I can only use power as a substitute for oxygen for so long." She threaded magic into her body to allow her to gather more air in case she wasn't able to escape quickly.

By the time they found the room where the pommel was located, the water was waist-deep. The object of their search rested on top of the stone coffin, held upright in the hands of the chiseled figure which, unlike those they'd seen before, was carved with meticulous detail. She grasped it but it refused to slide from the hold of its long-dead guardian. With a growl, she blasted the sarcophagus with force magic, shattered the stone, and pulled her prize free.

Her power activated a ward she hadn't detected. Two things happened almost simultaneously and overlapped in her senses, even though the one preceded the other by a scant second. A cage of magic slammed down around her to trap the interior of the room in a translucent cube only slightly smaller than the chamber itself. Fyre had stood outside its boundaries, which left her alone in the arcane prison. An instant later, the world lurched down and sideways and metal shrieked and groaned as the ship dropped from its moorings toward the chasm below.

Cali's feet lost purchase, and she slid to her left and impacted into the magical barrier hard enough to jar her brain out of its confused stasis. She searched her memory for the preparations they'd made before the initial swim to New Atlantis, and the process finally returned to her a little sluggishly. It took several moments for her to create the shield around her, extend it outward to trap the most air, and to use her magic to change the way her body used the oxygen. This time, it seemed more effective than before and she pushed the anxiety of suffocation out of her head for the moment.

The sounds of metal under strain increased, and a new worry emerged. Being crushed by the increasing pressure of the water would be no better than expiring from lack of air. She called to Fyre. *"Are you okay, buddy?"*

His telepathic response was reassuring. He sounded annoyed rather than worried. *"Fine. Outside the boat. It's breaking up in places."*

"Well, that's a positive but I bet this cage won't float. See if you can ice the part of the ship I'm in. Maybe we'll be able to find a weak place to break through."

"On it."

She had to grin at the way his speech patterns became more like hers the longer they communicated mentally.

They were definitely closer partners than they had ever been before. *Not that it's a huge help now.* She sifted through her escape options in quick sequence. *Fire, no. Lightning, hell no. Force, probably not. But what if I combined them?*

The idea blossomed within. She wedged herself into a corner of the cage, thankful that whoever had designed the trap hadn't made the surfaces painful. *They doubtless assumed drowning or being crushed was adequate. Well, I'll explain their error to them—in detail and over a long period of time.*

With a deep breath, she banished all nonessential thoughts to their alcoves in her mind and bound them in place with crime-scene tape. She imagined a cylinder of force that extended from her to the part of the room that currently faced up and ended where it made contact with the cage. Power pulsed into it to reinforce the boundaries. When it was solid, she pulled at all the magic inside her and summoned lightning. Cautiously, she channeled it through the confined path she'd created and hoped she had it corralled properly so it wouldn't spread and electrocute her.

The electricity surged free and attacked the structure that imprisoned her. Against an enemy who was present and could rebalance their defenses, it would have been futile. But she was able to drill through the ward, which had been placed who knew how long before. With extreme focus, she cut a hole in the barrier by directing her combined magics in a circle large enough to wiggle out of. When she had finished, she allowed the rest of the world into her senses and could almost feel the ship buckle around her.

"Are you ready, Fyre?"

"It's iced."

"Okay, then. Here goes." She blasted fire through the opening she'd created. The stressed metal, caught between cold and hot and under immense pressure, gave at the seams and a large piece fell away to reveal the ocean beyond. She waited while the room filled, safe in her personal cocoon, then swam out and up with the Draksa at her side.

When they finally resurfaced at the dock, she clambered onto the wooden platform and lay motionless for a moment, exhausted. Her companion stared at her from above and dripped water into her face. "Knock it off, long, wet, and scaly."

He grinned and shook to drench her again. "Okay. Your wish is my command, Matriarch." His imitation of the strange woman they'd spoken to on board was perfect.

Cali sighed. "We have more questions than answers after this trip. But we also have this." She held the hilt of her family's heirloom sword up. "And that makes all the effort worthwhile." Satisfied, she laid back and closed her eyes. "And when I find whoever stole it and hid it in there, I'll give them a close, personal look at the weapon they tried to keep from me."

CHAPTER THREE

Shenni swept down from the throne after a drudgery-filled afternoon of dealing with issues among her citizens. Gwyn was careful to ensure that only the problems that required her attention reached her and those with a complaint understood that the Empress's word was law. Despite the appropriate levels of fear and groveling the process produced, interacting with anyone under the level of the nobility simply no longer interested her. Too much was in motion too close to her position to focus beyond that.

She strode into her chambers and barely noticed the guards present at intervals along her path, other than to recognize that there seemed to be more of them than usual. *So Gwyn feels the strain too.* The city seemed to hold its breath, aware that a crisis was brewing, even though it hadn't yet broken out publicly. *Well, except for the ill-advised attack on Leblanc and Wymarc.* She shook her head. *He's pleasant to look at but sometimes, he's as stupid as he is beautiful.* While she'd thought it a good ploy at the time, in retrospect, it was more weight on the end of the scale that dipped toward chaos.

One by one, she stripped her garments off and dropped them on her way to the shower. Once there, she let the hot water beat down on her and tipped her head back so it could flow through her hair. The magical tentacles rocked gently under the spray, a sensation that never failed to calm her nerves. She stood under the stream for as long as she could until a knock on the door signaled the end of her free time.

With a sigh, she wrapped herself in towels and stepped out to where her seneschal and a servant waited. Gwyn smiled at her. "Do you feel better, Empress?"

Shenni snorted softly. "About as well as can be expected, given what lies ahead." The formal dinner was necessary but she didn't look forward to it. The situation had required her to ally with Styrris Malniet, but that didn't mean she had to like it. *Or him. I feel sorry for Matriarch Cormier.* Tonight, she'd have to deliver on commitments thus far only hinted at, alluded to, and otherwise specifically not committed herself to bringing to fruition.

Damn him for putting me in this position. Damn Caliste Leblanc for her role. Damn them all.

As she allowed the other women to dress her, she mused on her situation. The report that the Rivette mausoleum had sunk was troubling and the reason behind it doubly so. First, a significant amount of family history had been lost with the sinking of the ship that had contained the remains of her ancestors. They had survived the destruction of Old Atlantis, only for their remains to be lost as well because of the actions of a child. And second, the child had stumbled upon her little experiment. Hopefully, she hadn't completely understood what she'd seen.

The need for fully dependable underlings had driven the project from the start. It had begun immediately after she'd taken the throne and on the first day she realized that beyond Gwyn, anyone might act against her at any moment. The use of magic to influence others' minds had a long history. Her family's experiments had been to find a way to achieve full mastery with minimal effort. The collars acted to suppress the wearer's magic, which made them more vulnerable to control.

How I'd love to get one of those around Caliste's neck—and maybe Styrris's as well. The family member who had controlled the subjects reported only success, despite the loss of the entire project. It was only a matter of time before they created more collars and found more subjects, willing or unwilling. *Then I'll have a force I can trust completely and I'll be able to avoid nights like tonight.*

Gwyn stepped back and nodded. "You look perfect, Empress."

Shenni turned to face the mirror and had to admit that her closest confidant was correct. She was in a base dress of deep blue with a sleeved cape that reached almost to the floor. Elegant high heels in black were visible when she swayed and sent the material of dress and cape into motion. Her hair was piled perfectly on her head, and the minimal makeup the servant had added made her look subtly menacing, which was exactly how she felt. *Minus the subtle part.*

Styrris Malniet was waiting when she arrived in the smaller of her formal dining rooms. He rose and bowed but did not come to kiss her hand as protocol demanded. Of course, he would point to the rules of Old Atlantis, which did not require such deference toward the monarch. *Which is probably why it fell.*

She rewarded him with a frosty smile, lowered herself into her chair, and gestured for him to take his own. If he was intimidated by the guards at each corner of the room with their shining armor and tall tridents—or the knowledge he surely possessed that crossbows were aimed at him from behind the walls—it didn't show. He was a match to her elegance, dressed in a long green tunic with the stylized hook that was his family's symbol stitched into each cuff and over his heart in silver thread. His short dark hair and sharp features made him look like something trapped midway between a statesman and a cadaver.

Gwyn approached and poured wine for them, a deep red that looked like blood in the dim light thrown by the chandelier above. It was capable of more illumination, but she knew the Malniet Patriarch's eyes were diminished by age and it amused her to exploit that fact. She took a long sip, rolled the liquid in her mouth to appreciate the flavors, and swallowed with a smile. "So, Styrris. It is a pleasure to see you, as always."

His oily, self-satisfied smirk made her want to smack him. *If I didn't need you, you feckless sardine, you'd be a pincushion.* She visualized the man with crossbow bolts protruding from him everywhere and immediately felt better.

As always, his voice was as smooth as his expression. "I

appreciate the invitation, Empress, as always." She read the mockery in his tone easily and wondered if he'd ever fooled anyone or if he'd merely been so powerful that it didn't matter. *Careful. That could be the image he tries to project.*

The first course, a seafood soup in a clear broth, arrived immediately. They tasted it but neither ate more, both clearly focused on issues of greater import. She considered being oblique but discovered she lacked the energy for it. Instead, she asked, "What is your plan for getting rid of the girl?"

He shrugged. "I have one. However, it will remain inactive until such a time as we have agreements between us."

"You are bold."

A small laugh escaped him. "Some might see it so. My perspective is that it is simply an exchange where each party must bring equal value."

Shenni shook her head. "So what you're saying is that I'll have to pay to see your cards." He nodded. "Fine, then. To the matter at hand. I support your request to wed the matriarch of House Cormier." *Although I can't for the life of me understand why she'd want to attach herself to you.* "With the provision that the house itself continues in the hands of a relative until the current matriarch produces an heir."

The corners of his mouth turned down. "There are many worthy leaders among the members of my house."

"No. They have no bloodline connection except by your marriage, which is inadequate. We will not diminish the historical purity of the noble houses in such a way." She cared nothing for the details of her argument and only wished to be sure he was not able to put a lackey in place to lead Cormier.

His smile showed that he'd expected that outcome. *Which means he and the matriarch have something in mind. Well, naturally they do.* "Very well, Empress. I agree to those terms. However, that is not the entirety of my request."

She laughed and waited until the soup had been taken away and the entrée delivered to answer. "Of course it isn't. Please, tell me what else you require in order to do your duty and serve your city and your Empress as a noble should."

Amused at the sudden stillness in her dining partner, she lifted her utensils and sliced the thick slab of swordfish in front of her. *So you have at least a little sense of responsibility left in you. That is good to know.*

After a moment, he gathered himself with a nod of acknowledgment in her words. "Indeed, the tasks one is sometimes given require more effort than an ordinary subject could offer and thus should inspire more reward as well." He took a mouthful of his fish and chewed slowly before he swallowed. "I've noticed you do not have an heir, Empress."

Shenni pretended shock, but in her strategy sessions with Gwyn, they had envisioned this being an angle he might pursue. "Indeed, that is so. I'm still young, however, and have no lack of suitors wishing to supply me with one. Until your request to wed Cormier, I had wondered if you would eventually be among them." She continued to eat, content to let the silence stretch for as long as he could endure it.

After several moments, he finished his wine and raised

the glass for a refill. Gwyn was there in an instant, refreshed his drink, and turned her back to him to fill the Empress' cup. Her seneschal cut her gaze to the side of the room as if to ask for permission to have him shot, but she replied with a small headshake. *Not yet but maybe soon. He's altogether too full of himself.*

When the woman had resumed her position at the back wall, Styrris said, "I have no wish to be the power behind the throne, Empress. But I would ask that you consider elevating house Malniet to the top of the hierarchy in a contest for the throne should one occur."

"Are you suggesting I'm in danger, Patriarch?" She looked at him over the rim of her glass as she sipped the wine.

"Always, Empress. Such is the burden of the monarch, is it not?"

She laughed. "Indeed, Styrris, it is. So, I will do this much. I will put your house second, after Rivette. If you get rid of the girl." *And only until I replace House Leblanc with someone truly loyal and elevate them above you.*

He nodded. "That's acceptable. So, to the question of the Leblanc child. She has trapped herself inside the rules of ritual combat. We are not so hampered, and our reach is long indeed. She will be eliminated in short order."

"And once you do, I will be happy to announce your impending nuptials to the remainder of the Nine. Those who are left, that is, after our game comes to its end."

He raised an eyebrow. "I don't recall that being one of the conditions, Empress."

"As you said, Styrris, the rewards can be great but only when the tasks are complete. But, to sweeten the pot as it were, I will throw you the biggest wedding party New Atlantis has ever seen so all may envy your prowess."

He nodded. "Very well, Empress." He could do little else once she echoed his own words to him. She was under no illusion that he would keep all his commitments. Fortunately, that released her from any concern with fulfilling her own. *Now, Styrris, let the* real *games begin.*

Zeb looked over the packed common room and shook his head. There wasn't ever a particularly good time for him to leave the tavern in Janice's hands—or any hands other than his own— but he would have preferred a less crowded day. The atmosphere was uneasy and seemed ready to break into anger. *Or maybe that's simply me.*

He wiped the bar with a rag and hopped off the platform that ran behind it. The seconds ticked away in his head—the ability to unconsciously track time to the second had been drilled into him through countless training sessions and reinforced on an even larger number of adventures. Sometimes, calculating exactly how many moments it would take an enemy to nock an arrow was the difference between marching home victorious or riding home on a funeral cart. Now, his brain told him he needed to get ready for the arrival of the magical council.

The dwarf returned Janice's wave as he strode down the stairs. After a little telekinesis to move boxes out of the way and an incantation to release the wards, he pressed on the bricks that opened the secret door. None of those actions managed to improve his mood in the least. He paused and took a deep breath, seeking within for calm. When he was settled and ready again, he lit the fire in the hearth hurriedly and retrieved glasses for his guests.

They arrived one by one, as always, and each looked as concerned as he felt. The normal pre-meeting chatter was absent, and more than half the new arrivals drained their first glass and poured a second before the session had even begun. He took his seat last, as he usually did, in the only empty chair remaining. Vizidus was on his left and Delia on his right. The wizard seemed fully healed after his adventure against the traitorous magical who served the Zatoras, and the witch was her usual pleasantly abrasive self. The fury that blazed in her eyes, however, burned hotter today unless his vision failed him.

The white-haired leader of the council cleared his throat. *Okay, he sounds a little raspy still. Maybe he's not fully healed.* "Thank you for coming and thanks to Zeb, as always." The old man chuckled. "I have come to the inescapable conclusion that we need to stop dithering and act lest the sky fall upon us while we natter impotently."

Delia laughed loudly. She wore a long sweater dress, a rare departure from her normal jeans and sweatshirt look. It was a slightly darker black than her hair, which was braided and fell on either side of her neck like a schoolgirl's. "Or a ceiling is dropped on us, you mean?"

His laugh was darker but still held humor. "Or that, yes. We, as a group, may have been somewhat in denial about how directly this situation might affect us. I, at least, have been wholly disabused of that notion." Nods accompanied the statement from almost everyone in the room.

The Kilomea was the next to speak. Brukirot's arms were folded over his massive chest but his expression was neutral. He seemed no more or less affronted than on any other day. "So, can we finally all agree that it's time to act?" The warlike giant had been in favor of intervention from the moment they'd discovered the rising danger in New Orleans.

Scoppic, the gnome librarian, was in his traditional light-colored suit. His round glasses were slightly askew. "I've received an invitation to visit New Atlantis and assist Caliste's great-aunt with her research. I plan to go as soon as I can arrange things with my colleagues at the library."

Zeb grinned. "Cali will appreciate that." The normal boundaries of taking turns to speak based on their position at the table seemed unnecessary given the clear need for the council's involvement. Their focus was now more on deciding how to do it than arguing over whether they should.

Invel, the Drow, replied, "I believe I shall join you, my friend. We three can doubtless make a significant differ-ence in the situation from there." The dwarf smothered his smile, reluctant to reveal his friend's romantic interest in Emalia to anyone who didn't already know it. *Somehow, I thought you'd wind up there before too much time had passed.*

Which was not to say that the Dark Elf wouldn't be an invaluable asset. He absolutely would and that was the best place for his particular set of skills. But for people like Zeb, whose talents ran in a more decidedly martial direction, the picture was not quite as clear.

Malonne, in many ways the opposite of Invel with his light skin and elegant features, asked, "And what should the rest of us do? Is it open war, magical against magical, for the prize of the city? And if we win, what then? Simply let the humans continue as always?" He shook his head. "It does not seem to me that they have done an effective job thus far. Perhaps we should be the ones in charge henceforth."

It had been a long time since the Light Elf had last made that argument. It had not garnered much support then but now, the expressions around the table were interested rather than dismissive.

Zeb frowned. "Maybe we should deal with the situation in front of us instead of trying to jump forward a dozen steps."

The other man raised a long-fingered hand in a conciliatory gesture. Vizidus wore a frown as he asked, "Is there anyone present who believes we should not act at this time?" When no responses followed, he continued. "Excellent. Now, we must decide what form that intervention should take. Scoppic and Invel have chosen their paths. I will coordinate our activities and reach out to allies in other cities. Delia, what are your plans?"

The dark-haired witch leaned back in her chair. "First off, I'll take care of my people. We're working together to ward our homes and businesses. Once that's done, count me in for whatever kind of havoc we want to wreak on the Zatoras, the Atlanteans, or whoever else is causing trouble. But I'm not interested in a stand-up fight. They don't play fair and I won't either. If that's a problem for anyone, I'll fly solo."

Brukirot shrugged. "I will take the battle any way it comes but my best role is the hunter. Find me the right targets and this situation will be ended quickly."

Malonne laughed. "As if the right targets haven't been obvious all along. The leadership of the gangs. Surely you don't need assistance to find them." His mocking tone made Zeb's hands clench involuntarily. "And perhaps add the human leaders of the city to that list, given their clear inability to manage the protection of their citizens."

The dwarf shook his head. "Rhazdon's atrocities showed the error of thinking ourselves superior simply because we possess magic. We need to partner with those around us, not look for opportunities to knock them down." The scowl he received from the Light Elf at the mention of the ancient Oriceran villain soothed him. "I will continue to run the tavern and welcome clients of every kind. I can also act as the connection between the council and Cali and thus to the happenings in New Atlantis."

Vizidus knocked on the table to draw their attention. "Very well. It seems we all have our immediate tasks to perform. Malonne, perhaps you could take the same precautions as Delia for your people. In fact, we all should." He shook his head. "It would be easy to think that this isn't our problem but it is. Either gang taking power over the other would be bad for everyone in the city. The best plan is to try to eliminate both and do the same to anyone else who thinks they're in a position to rule over those who have no wish to be ruled."

More nods followed. Zeb's anxiety faded into a certainty that the group was on the right path and would stay on that route as long as the old wizard was in charge. "Okay, so we have a plan," he said. "That's good. Use the tavern as an escape whenever you need to. I'll be here twenty-four-seven until the situation is resolved. There will always be food, drink, and medical supplies for whoever needs it." He swiveled his head to regard the Dark Elf. "Invel, will you set us up with extra potions before you leave?"

"Of course. You can have anything you might think useful. I won't do any trading while I'm in New Atlantis. That I know of." The thoughtful look on his face suggested that he had some hopes in that area and Zeb stifled a chuckle. *You always have an angle, my friend, and we're all the better for it.*

The witch rose and stretched. "Good. The plans are good. Our best guess is that it'll take us a couple of days to get all our responsibilities locked down. After that, I'll be ready for other tasks and can probably convince a few friends to come along as well. But remember, we need to be a scalpel, not a hammer."

Brukirot grinned. "But hammers are so much more effective."

She rolled her eyes and gave him a slap on the shoulder as she headed to the back of the room to portal away. The Kilomea followed her as he stated, "I'm ready now. When you choose a target, let me know." Malonne and Scoppic departed next, the former with an air of hostility and the latter with a decided aura of excitement. Zeb stood and collected the remaining members' glasses, refilled them, and returned to the table.

"So," he said. "Maybe we waited too long."

Vizidus sighed. "There's no way to be sure, even in hindsight, that we could have made a difference before now. The Zatoras and the Atlanteans have created risks for themselves—and an opportunity for us—by focusing so completely on one another. The smarter move would have been to agree to share the city."

Invel chuckled. "Even we at this table are not all good at sharing. It is no surprise that the others are no better."

The dwarf pulled his pipe out, lit it, and smoked thoughtfully for a moment. "The key here, like Delia says, is to be surgical. We certainly don't want to garner any more attention. Let them both think we've been driven into hiding by the attack on one of our own. Then, we can watch and wait for an opportunity to shift the balance."

"In which direction, though?" the Dark Elf asked. "Is one better than the other?"

Vizidus shook his head. "No. If we're to turn our efforts to repulsing the encroachment from New Atlantis, they both have to go. But we must be wary. Eliminating the weaker may allow the stronger to stabilize. No, we need to keep them both active until the very last moment, when we can wipe both of them from the board."

Invel pushed to his feet and limped toward the rear of the room. "I will be in New Atlantis, but I stand ready to assist in any way necessary. Just let me know. Zeb, in say two hours, I'll portal back and we can move things out of my shop?"

Zeb nodded, and his friend stepped through the rift in space and vanished. He sighed. "Well, Vizidus, I wouldn't want your job but I'm glad you're the one doing it."

The wizard laughed. "I already feel a decade younger.

Who knows? By the end of this, I might agree with Malonne. What do you think? Would I make a good mayor?" He struck a noble pose and his friend snorted.

"Brukirot would get more votes."

He scowled in response. "I'd be offended, but you're no doubt right. Troubling times are ahead. Still, we'll meet them and come out the other side stronger for the trial."

The dwarf nodded and lifted his glass to drain it. *Here's hoping all of us make it through, but if only one gets to, I'll do everything in my power to make sure it's Cali.*

CHAPTER FIVE

Ozahl stepped through the portal from a neutral location into the lobby of the Zatora gang's new headquarters. Unknown to most of the city, the gang had acquired several small hotels in the French Quarter through shell companies and had evicted all the guests from one of them after the events at the mansion. The building was now locked to the outside world and secured by guards at every entrance.

The Zatora leader had taken the top of the three floors for himself and the mage was required to pass through three different groups of armed guards to reach him, even though he was expected.

He's decided not to take any more chances. It's a good choice, but it won't save him unless he makes the most difficult decision of all and cancels the funeral.

That was highly unlikely except in extreme circumstances, and if he began to lean in that direction, it would be up to him to nudge him back on track. To bring the gang together out in the open was the culmination of a long series of events and he wasn't about to let that much effort go to waste.

Besides, if there's any human who deserves to have his time in this life shortened, it's Rion Grisham.

He found the boss in a room that had seen the removal of its beds and the addition of a table and chairs to turn it into a meeting space. The shades were drawn to block the afternoon sunlight. The only illumination was from a chandelier that had to be at least a half-century old and probably more, which was entirely inadequate to fill the area. Shadows gathered in the corners of the room and under the eyes of the two men who awaited him inside it.

At the far end of the table, farthest from the door, Rion Grisham's face was flat and expressionless. In Ozahl's experience, the less emotion he showed, the more dangerous he was. His hair was perfectly slicked back and his suit immaculate.

Clearly, he's seeking to control everything he can, which honestly isn't all that much.

To his left, Jack Strang glowered. His bald head shined like he'd oiled it, but his face held the stubble of at least a day without shaving. His countenance was as volatile as Grisham's was passive. The man likely had doubts about how his friend Colin Todd had met his demise but, given the lack of proof, the risk that his involvement could be confirmed was minimal.

Ozahl sat and gave the lieutenant a nod before he faced the boss. "The streets are quiet and there is no evidence that the magical gang or council is causing trouble. Our people are going about their business without opposition."

Grisham growled belligerently. "Which is as suspicious as hell."

Strang nodded. "Entirely. Why wouldn't someone take advantage of this moment?"

The mage shrugged. "Maybe they fear a trap. They don't know how resilient we might be." *It always feels weird saying "we" to these people.* "It's not like we haven't delivered both Leblanc and the Atlanteans some seriously unexpected blows in the recent past."

The Zatora leader shook his head. "No, they're waiting for us to show ourselves so they can strike. Well, at least those of us who don't have magical disguises to rely upon." Anger bubbled through his words but Ozahl didn't think it was directed at him.

Strang coughed and said, "Which is why we shouldn't go through with it, boss. Colin wouldn't care."

"No. It's not for him. It's for our people. They need to see that we won't be cowed. Our enemies attacked us in our place." He shouted the last two words as his outrage exploded from him but made an obvious effort to control himself. "So, we won't let fear stop us from doing what needs to be done. We'll have the funeral but we'll plan for the worst."

Ozahl shook his head. "Strang's right, Rion. This isn't smart." *That should counter any suspicion of me somewhat.*

"Smart or not, we're doing it. Now, we have to decide how to do it properly." He pointed at the other man in the room. "Jack, you're in charge of dealing with physical security. What do you think we'll need?"

The big man sighed. "Where will we have it?"

Grisham's grin was like a knife slash. "St. Louis."

Strang's eyes widened, and even Ozahl was taken aback by the audacity of the choice. The security lieutenant said, "Are you serious? That's a nightmare when it comes to controlling the space."

"I've never been more serious. We have to make it a show. For our people, sure, but for the Atlanteans and every person in New Orleans as well. And that includes the bloody magical council. Not only are we undeterred, we're rushing back stronger than ever."

The mage shook his head. "That's definitely bold. We'll need more people. A lot more people."

Grisham nodded. "They are already on their way. Our numbers will be doubled by Saturday and more will arrive in time for the event on Sunday night."

Across from him, the other man muttered, "We'll need to put every damn one of them on patrol outside the venue and have sharpshooters inside."

The boss waved a hand dismissively. "Do whatever you need to do. Give me a summary once a day. I trust you to get it right." Left unsaid was that they doubtless thought they'd gotten it right at the mansion, too. Grisham asked, "And what will you do for magical security?"

Ozahl shrugged. *Make sure there are enough holes in it to get you killed, that's what.* "I can only do so much, so we'll have to rely on Strang's people as an outer cordon. If they keep everyone away, that will include magical threats. I will put wards up to give us a warning if there's magic being used within a certain radius of the building. The problem is it'll have to happen on the day of the event since we can't risk giving the game away." He shook his head. "I'll work out the best way to achieve that and I'll be positioned close by in case. Of course, that won't stop something like the Kraken that attacked the docks from showing up and ruining our day."

The gang leader's smile was bloodthirsty. "The new folks will bring firepower with them, which includes more anti-magic bullets. I think we'll be able to handle anything they throw at us as long as they get close enough."

"That's good to know." *Especially for Danna and Usha.* "I'll focus on making sure they can't attack from far away—expand the wards and position myself outside, at least at the start, where I can keep an eye on things."

The boss nodded. "That sounds logical. Now, there's one other thing we need to consider. The girl. She's bound to show up." When Ozahl had revealed to the others that Caliste Leblanc had been part of the attack, their rage had been enormous. They'd given her equal weight as the Atlanteans, which served his purposes perfectly.

Misdirection is the key, as any good magician will tell you.

Strang growled his animosity. "I'll have someone on each side watching for her. We'll kill her before she gets within a hundred feet."

Ozahl shook his head. "That's not adequate. She can come in under a veil or in a disguise. There's no way you can identify her. You know that civilians will inevitably show up to gawk at the funeral and we can't keep them out if you really want to make a show of force. No, we'll need something more subtle for her."

"Eliminate the dwarf?" Grisham asked. "Use him as a hostage? Or maybe her karate teacher?"

"She's in tight with the council now. If we do that, we're bound to wind up with all of them against us rather than operating as a disorganized muddle of morons. No, I don't think that's a good play. If she's stupid enough to show her face, we can use the innocents in the room as leverage against her. But it would be incredibly foolish of her to risk it. I doubt she'll do it." *But oh, if she did, it would be a beautiful thing.*

"I hope she does," Strang blurted. "That witch needs to die and I want to be the one to do it."

Grisham chuckled. "Take a number. I'm fairly sure we'd all like to put at least one bullet in her. If we're lucky, we can capture her and let our resident interrogator spend quality time with her." He nodded toward the mage. "In any case, get your plans together. We'll meet here every night." He rose and strode from the room, and the sound of a nearby door closing came a moment later.

Ozahl looked at the man across from him. "You know this is a terrible idea, right?"

"Yeah. But it's the boss' call. You do your part and I'll do mine. Somehow, we'll make it work."

His nod covered the satisfaction he felt inside at the continued smooth operation of his plan. *No, my esteemed colleague, I don't think you will.*

He had been home for more than an hour before Danna portaled into the closet. With a smile, he bounded from the bed and greeted her at the doorway that separated the small area from the bedroom. "Hello, love." She looked beautiful in her dark suit and slicked-down short hair.

Even under the light makeup she always wore, she seemed tired.

She gave him a weary grin. "Hello yourself." She put a hand on his chest and pushed him slowly back until he fell onto the mattress, then flopped beside him. Her voice was muffled by the fact that her face was pressed into the comforter. "How was your day?"

He laughed. "Eventful. Our friend Rion is well aware that there are security risks involved with the funeral but determined to hold it just the same."

She rolled onto her back and expelled a lungful of air. "Good. That's good. Usha and I will start planning the attack in earnest tomorrow. I presume they'll bring in extra troops and ring the location?"

"You got it."

"Is it where we thought it would be?"

Ozahl laughed. "Of course. His ego could never choose anything other than the most visible church in all of New Orleans."

Danna grinned. "It's so comforting when people act exactly the way you expect them to."

"Speaking of which, do you think Leblanc will show up? Grisham does. I don't."

She raised her hands for a moment and let them fall onto the bed. "There's no reason for her to unless we want to give her a little nudge. But she's one of our options to use in New Atlantis, so that would be dumb on our part."

"It would be satisfying, though."

"No one wants to see her defeated as much as I do." She laughed and it sounded a little brittle. "I'm sick of being on the losing team but we need to keep our eye on the prize. At least that's what my partner always tells me."

He pushed onto an elbow to look at her. "He sounds like a smart person."

Danna closed her eyes and smiled. "He's all right."

The day's demand for planning and plotting fulfilled, he covered her lips with his and pushed everything other than the woman he adored out of his mind.

CHAPTER SIX

Usha had already tried to spend time at her desk, stretched on the couch in her office, or even seated in the concealed nook she used to commune with the Empress. None of it relieved the restless energy that called her to action. She ventured into the main room and was assaulted by a wall of noise. For her patrons, workers, and the band, it was all business as normal.

But nothing is normal for me. Everything is in the air and I don't know where any of it will land.

The worst part of it was that, for the first time in memory, she no longer possessed purity of purpose. Her last visit to the Empress had left her off-center and each day since had exacerbated the feeling. She couldn't begin to guess at the why of Shenni's actions, but the fact of them felt like a betrayal. And with that essential support shaken, all her efforts on the surface suddenly seemed far less important. It was a moment by moment battle to maintain her image in front of her people. This was such a fundamental problem that she couldn't even share it with Danna.

She slid onto a barstool and gestured for a drink. The Pina Colada appeared in moments as if they'd known she was coming and had started it before she arrived. She accepted it gratefully and sipped it, then pulled the pineapple wedge from the lip of the glass and tore it from the skin with her teeth. The band segued from jazz into swing, and people flowed toward the dance floor.

Maybe I should simply become a club owner. I bet I would be good at it.

The gang leader was so absorbed in her thoughts that she had no warning of the other woman's presence before she sat beside her.

"I'll have what she's having," Danna called. Her second in command tilted her head to the side and stared at her. "You look perplexed."

"That's one word for it, I guess." She laughed. "How are things on the streets?" Her place right now was at the Shark Nightclub coordinating the efforts of others despite how much she'd rather be out making things happen.

Her companion shrugged. Her navy-blue suit was perfect, as always, and she'd chosen a black shirt and purple tie to accompany it. Usha wasn't sure how she managed to keep it looking pressed all day and often wondered if she used magic to do it. "The usual. People are upset about the reduced quantities of both Zarcanum and Shine, and we're redirecting their anger toward the Zatoras. I'd say the battle of opinion is trending toward our side if that matters."

Usha tapped one nail on the bar. "It all matters. How much, only time will tell. Would you say things are stable?"

Danna nodded. "That's unacceptable. We want people angry at the Zatoras. Let's push harder. Tomorrow, decrease the Zarcanum even more and remove any of the dealers on the street. We need to add stress to the situation so if something does break, it goes in the right direction."

Surprise registered on the other woman's face. "Are you sure? That's likely to cause things to boil over."

She sighed. "I'm tired of playing this game with them. Sunday, one way or another, this fight has to be brought to an end."

"Okay, boss, you're the brains of the operation." Danna flashed her a smile. "And what do you want to do about Matriarch Caliste?"

That drew a short laugh from her boss. "Well, if the universe is kind, she'll be swept up in the action at the funeral and we won't have to deal with her anymore. But since that's not something we can depend on, I guess we need to come up with another plan. What do you think?"

"I say we wrap it up. Make her an offer she won't be able to refuse and advance the final battle. She has to be as tired of it all as we are and we can't afford the distraction any longer."

While she drained the rest of her drink and signaled for another, she considered her subordinate's words. They were appealing on several levels. If the move against the Zatoras went as they hoped, the girl would be one of the last potential obstacles to securing control of the city. Admittedly, the magical council would be a challenge, but they could be convinced to join in a beneficent ruling coalition under the authority of New Atlantis. The girl was the wild card and getting her out of the way was an important step to finally achieving their purpose.

It would take the combat ritual off the table and free resources and energy for other tasks, which was another plus. The only downside was that the girl might win, which would be entirely unacceptable to the Empress as that would mean no one associated with the gang could touch her thereafter. If they chose to go that route, it would require fielding the best they had.

When her drink arrived, Usha responded with a word of thanks and shifted her gaze to her companion. "Okay. I agree. It's time to bring it to an end. That's our first task after the funeral. If there are any logistics to plan, get started as soon as possible."

The other woman nodded and stood from her stool. She rested a hand on her boss' shoulder and leaned close to whisper in her ear as applause filled the room and the band departed for their intermission. "We've got this. Don't worry. All the pieces will fall into place exactly like they should, and we'll come out the other side on top."

Danna strode away and left only the musky scent of her perfume to accompany Usha's musings. She sipped her drink as she put the individual components of her mental puzzle into various positions to see how they fit best. By the time she was finished, she was resolved. Even though what she intended to do now had always been a last resort part of the plan, in this unique moment, she had the power to tilt the playing surface under everyone's feet and gain an advantage by implementing it.

She emptied the glass and placed it on the bar. When the bartender arrived and asked if she wanted a refill, she shook her head. She had a different request. "Call Mia and Tia. Tell them I need them here in an hour."

The Atlantean gang leader had used the intervening time to prepare for the ritual. While she understood the magic she intended to cast, she had never done so on the kind of scale that would be required now. Even though her power was strong—powerful enough to help her rise to become Champion of New Atlantis—this would require more.

She feared it would require everything she had to give, which was why Danna wasn't present. If something went wrong, at least the task given to them by the Empress could be completed under her second in command's leadership. Whether or not Shenni still had faith in her, she intended to do her best to see her ruler's vision realized.

The office had been transformed into a ritual area. Objects of power were present at each cardinal point, from a tiny seashell passed down from Old Atlantis to the basin she used to commune with her ruler. They would amplify what went on within it. All the furniture had been pushed out of the way save the two couches, which now faced one another in the center of the room with barely enough space between them for her to fit.

The last ten minutes were about centering herself. Usha put on the dress she had only ever worn to speak to the Empress and bound her hair in a hasty braid that hung down her back. She applied the makeup she thought of as her war paint—the deep scarlet symbols that had carried her through the ritual battles during her rise. Stripes were painted on each cheek, one for Old Atlantis and one for New. The wings of a stingray across her forehead came next. A shark's tooth was deftly portrayed on her chin. Her personal weapons from that time, unfortunately, were on display in the palace as a reminder of her success.

At the appointed moment, the door to the office opened and the twins stepped in. The women were young, barely past the age of choice in New Atlantis and a year away from starting their third decade. Both were dark with black hair and shining eyes. They had something distinctly otherworldly about them, which was what had brought them to the Empress's attention and then to Usha's. It had been difficult to persuade the sisters to come to the surface but she'd managed it with promises of a quick rise through the ranks to positions of power.

If any of them survived the night, she would make good on that commitment. Such an outcome was far from guaranteed, however. The twins read the gravity of the situation instantly and did not speak as they moved to the couches when she pointed to where she wanted them. They reclined and she knelt between them and stretched her hands out to grasp a wrist of each of them. She closed her eyes and focused her mind, then began her work.

The first step was to break down the barriers between herself and her partners. Since they were young and comparatively unskilled, it would have to be a one-way flow in which she pulled from them but didn't permit them to ride that channel into her mind. She'd done it before to replenish her strength between bouts but it had been a while. Fortunately, her magic remembered. In minutes, the women were open reservoirs of power for her to draw on.

If only the whole process was that easy. She shifted her weight to find the most comfortable position, unsure of how long she'd have to hold it. Satisfied, she tuned the physical sensations out and descended completely into the mental space where her magic lived. When they'd included the magic component in each of the new drugs, she had spent hours attuning herself to it in preparation for this moment.

She sent her power outward in a circle in search of the magical signature. The first reflections came from the main room of her club. There were only a couple, which meant that at least one high-roller able to afford Zarcanum was amongst the crowd. She almost quailed and pulled back from taking the action she'd deemed essential. But weakness of will had never stopped her before and she wouldn't allow it to on this occasion either. Usha quashed those feelings and activated the latent power. It would take time for the spark to grow but the cycle was now in motion.

Resolved, she pressed her power farther outward and drew energy from the women beside her, who moaned in protest but were too drained to do anything to hinder it. The magic inside her pressed at her ability to control it but again, long-developed discipline prevailed. It was mere moments before she found the first Shine user and activated that magic as well. The knowledge that both drugs had responded as expected settled something in her chest.

Now, it's only a matter of whether I'm strong enough to reach everyone in the city. Her mind held no doubt on that score. If it cost all three of them their lives, she would see it accomplished. Soon, the magicals would find their power draining as the drug pulled at their magic. The additive in the human version would increase its users' emotional volatility. Chaos would ensue for a time, during which the Atlantean gang would focus on the Zatoras and the girl. But after, when the dust settled, the city would be ripe for new leadership. Her leadership.

CHAPTER SEVEN

Cali had managed a couple of shifts at the Drunken Dragons but had given her Thursday night hours to Janice because Nylotte had made her an offer she couldn't refuse. She'd run most of the way from the tunnel to the sword maker's shop and only slowed as she approached to catch her breath so she wouldn't display weakness in front of him. She was dressed for action in her uniform boots, dark jeans, and a long-sleeved black shirt.

She had no doubt that she'd fail in any number of other interesting ways during the training session they had planned for after she dropped the pommel off, so she didn't want to do that there too. Alessand's door was unlocked and she entered to find him seated on a high stool near the center island, reading from a very large book that appeared to be from a time long past judging by its heavy leather cover and yellowed pages. Diagrams of swords and extended swaths of text in an alphabet she didn't recognize covered the tome.

He gave her a welcoming smile and when he saw the object she carried, it widened into a grin of delight. His voice was smooth and almost desirous. "What have you brought me, Matriarch Leblanc?"

"A little something that should make the whole reforging process easier." She grinned in return, set the black velvet bundle on the table, and gestured for him to examine it. Alessand unfolded the fabric carefully as if he wanted to stretch the experience as long as possible. When he had finished, the hilt of the Leblanc family sword lay before them, as pristine as if it had just been created. The gem that shone in the pommel was a flawless turquoise, notable in part because that particular stone was rarely found in water.

He dragged in an awed breath. "It's beautiful."

Cali nodded. "Like a piece of history."

He lifted the item and examined it in the light that filtered from the lamp hanging above the island. The gemstones glittered as he turned the pommel and he pointed to a line of script. "What does that say?"

She frowned and squinted to make the letters out but couldn't translate them. "I'm not sure. When Emalia's done with all her other tasks, I'll ask her to have a look at it."

"That's understandable." He laughed. "Certainly, you have things to do other than investigate your ancestry." Almost regretfully, he folded the item into its wrappings. "Will you acquire the remaining pieces soon?" He couldn't hide the note of hope, excitement, or maybe avarice in his voice.

"I plan to. It's one of my highest priorities. Right after survival, more or less."

"It seems as if your issues are in the proper order then."

"I'd like to think so. Anyway, I have to get moving or Nylotte will make me pay for it."

His grin returned. "Ah, indeed. One should never disappoint her. She has a long memory."

She sensed a story but lacked time to inquire. Instead, she bolted from the shop with a wave and ran to the front of the Dark Elf's home and business. She paused to suck in a deep breath and stepped inside. Immediately, the other woman's voice floated up from the basement. "You're late."

Cali rolled her eyes and shut the door, then made her way down the stairs. "Am not. I'm perfectly on time."

The Drow was seated in a lotus position in the center of the warding circle. Her outfit was all dark and almost identical to her own but of much finer quality. She raised an elegant eyebrow at her student's arrival. "Which is late. Didn't your great-aunt teach you proper manners?"

In silence, she sat across from her and bound her hair back with a tie before she responded. "Yeah, but you know, some lessons don't take as well as others. Zeb makes a similar complaint from time to time."

Nylotte laughed. "He is a man of considerable patience to deal with you on such a regular basis."

With a sigh, she replied, "Are you this abusive to all your students?"

"Only the ones I like."

"You have students you dislike?"

She grinned and showed her teeth. "They rarely last long."

"I'll pretend you simply mean they choose to no longer

be taught by you. Please don't bother to correct me. So, what's the plan?"

The Dark Elf nodded and turned businesslike but didn't bother to hide the amused sparkle in her eye. *At least she's not kicking me out or whatever. Yet.*

"There are three things you need to learn based on what I've seen and been told by Diana. First, to master lightning. Second, how to use others' magic as fuel. Third, how to properly swing a sword."

Cali frowned. "I have more than enough magic and Sensei Ikehara says I'm fine with a sword."

Her teacher shook her head. "Fine is not good enough. And with all appropriate respect to your martial arts instructor, my techniques have been refined by practical experience. You will benefit from the additional knowledge."

"I bow to your great wisdom."

Nylotte uncoiled into a standing position in a smooth motion that her student envied. Jealousy wasn't a good trainer, however, so she rose and threw her jacket outside the circle, then turned her full attention to the other woman, who spoke without delay.

"So, you have managed to force the lightning to do your bidding at other times. Now, you will convince it, instead."

Sure I will. "Okay."

Her tone must have conveyed the doubt because the Drow repeated, "You will. Believe it."

"I'm ready."

"Now, you'll do three things. First, you'll draw the energy out of you and create a shield of lightning all around you. That's the easy part as it already wants to come out. You simply need to tell it to stop afterward." The other woman stepped outside the ring and gestured, and a shimmering cylinder rose to surround her student and reached to the ceiling.

Cali took a deep breath to focus and gave in to the constant pressure of her magic trying to escape. She transformed the raw power into electricity and let it slip a little before she pulled it back. It resisted like a pet straining against a leash. Instead of countering the impulse with force, she drew upon her martial arts mindset and redirected the energy to spin around her.

Her teacher clapped from her safe place outside the shield. "Well done. I've never seen one move like that before. It's a very interesting technique."

"Shut it," she muttered, then spoke loudly enough for the other woman to hear, "Okay, what's next?"

"Stop your whining. Okay, draw all that power into your hands. Later, you'll be able to skip the whole-body step, but it teaches an important mental part of the process. Imagine the lightning coating your skin the same way you've used force to do before. It's like a glove a centimeter away from the surface. If you need to make it move, that's fine."

Her voice was teasing at the end and made the girl smile even through the frustration of trying to learn the new magic that seemed so foreign to her. When Emalia had described it as forcing the lightning to do her bidding, that had made sense. This approach—coaxing and cajoling and essentially begging her power to do what she wanted it to do—somehow didn't seem natural.

But maybe what's natural isn't necessarily what's best, right? Natural didn't get me lightning whips.

She visualized her objective and her skin crawled as the lightning coalesced around her fists. With a chuckle, Nylotte said, "We're not forcing it, and you're not about to punch anyone. Relax." She obeyed and her hands ached as she forced them to unclench. "Now, imagine the power spilling forward toward the floor without losing your connection to it. Create the weapon you want."

Cali closed her eyes and pictured the whips, each about five feet, extending from her palms to coil on the ground near her boots. When she opened them, her vision had become a reality. She lifted one carefully and flicked it experimentally. It wavered and for a moment, she feared she was about to lose control of it before it solidified again. A few moments later, she had it and slashed the air with her new toys, a fierce grin on her face.

Nylotte dropped the shield and threw in a sphere of light, and Cali struck it with a snap of her wrist. Her teacher challenged her with more throws, and she intercepted each one. Finally, the woman said, "Okay, enough."

With a satisfied sigh, she let the magic fall away. "Not bad. Not bad at all. It only required a totally different perspective than any I've used before."

"That's all?" The Drow's tone was amused. "Well, good job with it anyway. You'll need to practice often in order to maintain them during a fluid situation like a battle, but I have no doubt you'll get there. Now, conjure a shield."

Over the next half hour, the Dark Elf instructed her how to siphon power with her shields rather than simply absorb or deflect it. She couldn't imagine a scenario where she'd need to use the technique but was glad to know it, nonetheless. By the time they'd finished, her mind was tired and she was aching from the constant push and pull of magic. She groaned and the Dark Elf laughed. "Yes, if you're sore, it means we've done a good job so far. Adapting your body to the demands of your magic is more difficult than it seems at first."

"I believe that. So, are you serious about the sword?"

"I am." Nylotte crossed into the storage area of the shop and returned with two wooden blades, each about the size of the heirloom that Alessand was restoring for her. She tossed one to Cali and spun the other through a complicated pattern of figure eights, circles, and slashes.

The hilt was worn as if it had been used to train countless students, and she was struck again by how many secrets lingered around the other woman. She made a mental note to chat to Diana about her as the agent would doubtless have a wealth of information to share. The weapon was a little heavy for one-handed use so she grasped the hilt with both.

Her teacher shook her head. "You'll need to be able to wield it one-handed. For now, you can practice with two as you'll want to have the option to do both. But you either have to build your muscles or use your magic because the other hand will be used for casting or defense."

She frowned. "You don't think I'll be able to cast magic through my family's sword?"

The Drow shrugged. "There's no record of that ability that Alessand or I could find so we can't count on it. If you can, it simply means we can put a shield or dagger in your off-hand. Either way, you need the flexibility. Trapping both your hands on one weapon would be extremely foolish." She moved into a fighting stance with the sword crossed before her. "Now, defend yourself if you can."

As Nylotte darted forward and the weapon swung, Cali threw her best block up, knowing there was no chance it would be in time. *Something tells me I'll regret this in the morning.*

CHAPTER EIGHT

The image that rippled on the other side of the portal was as strange as any place Cali had ever seen. With a nod to Nylotte and a grimace at the way her muscles hurt after the training session of the night before, she stepped from Earth to Oriceran and from the underground Kemana to the abandoned village the Drow had scouted for her.

The tear in reality closed behind her. The Dark Elf had offered to join her but this seemed like a task she needed to do alone, which was why she'd rejected the same offer from Tanyith, Zeb, and Fyre. Whether for herself, out of respect for her parents, or for some other reason, it didn't matter. She'd handle this particular investigation herself.

And, if something unexpected happens, I'll portal out and bring friends next time.

When her teacher had described the location as an abandoned village, Cali had imagined an image from *The Hobbit*—a cheerful community like the Shire. This was not even close. The homes were simple affairs of rough stone and cracked mortar. Freestanding barns suggested livestock or horses but nothing remained to indicate what might have once lived there. She'd thought of the location as a place people had recently moved on from. Instead, the town was cold, harsh, and utterly lifeless. Reflexively, she let her magic extend beyond the confines of her skin to detect any arcane danger before it could reach her.

If there had once been decorations or creature comforts of any kind, they were long gone. She shuddered at the unreality of the experience as she'd never seen a location on Earth like it and doubted she ever would. She pulled the map the Dark Elf had provided out of the back pocket of her combat uniform, oriented herself in the right direction, and stowed it again. An act of will summoned her sticks to her hands. Wary that this could be a trap, she strode forward.

The rest of the village was the same. A dozen or so families might have called the settlement home once upon a time, maybe more if they didn't live by the same social rules that were considered normal on her planet. Eventually, the individual buildings gave way to what had probably been the town square and the large structure positioned at the far end of it. That was her objective—the town's common building. She couldn't hazard a guess as to why her parents had selected that location. Her inclination would have been to choose the least impressive part of the community rather than the most obvious one.

Although it was constructed of the same mismatched stones as the rest of the village, it rose twice as high. The entry doors were also double the height of those in the homes and appeared to be solid as she approached them cautiously. She nudged her magic farther outward to seek wards or other dangers but detected none. Still, caution ruled her and she pushed on the doors with her sticks rather than touching them.

They swung open with only a whisper of protest to reveal an empty room beyond. In the center, a circle of stones surrounded a dark area with a place for the fire's smoke to escape in the ceiling above. The image of a community coming together there at night, parents and children, cooking and sharing stories and generally being with one another, rippled in her mind's eye.

Me? Emotional about family? Nah. She sniffed at the thought and moved toward the far end of the space, where a divider that stretched across three-quarters of the building's width separated the back portion.

Smaller doorways set in the side walls provided entry and exit, and low stone tables that she guessed were for food prep filled most of the area. What caught her attention was the section of the floor made of wood instead of stone. The heavy planks were as rough as the rest of the structure but they had one very compelling feature—a tall wooden ring that jutted from the center.

Cali tried unsuccessfully to lift it, pushed power into her muscles with magic, and failed again. She crouched beside the wood square in thought, then joined her sticks into a staff and pushed it through the handle. The lever plus her enhanced strength were sufficient to pop the cover free, and she let it fall to one side.

She directed a small ball of flame through the opening. The fire illuminated a short ladder leading to a basement that was barely higher than she was tall. "This doesn't look promising," she muttered but descended carefully. She directed the sphere around the cramped area—which was only slightly larger than the living room in her apartment —and found nothing other than the packed dirt floor under her feet and the stone walls on all four sides. Disappointment welled within her but she pushed it away.

The dagger had to have led me here for a reason. She examined each of the walls—first with her eyes, then with her magic, and finally, ran her fingertips in slow exploration over the surface and pressed inward.

By the time she had completed the two sides and made it halfway through the back one, she had begun to feel a little despondent when she found something new. A slender opening, more tall than wide, was hidden from view by a clever shadow cast by the surrounding stone. If she'd relied only on vision, she wouldn't have discovered the crevice. With growing excitement, she pulled the dagger out and pushed the tip into the gap. It slid fully into place with only the hilt on the outside. She waited but nothing happened. "Well, that's anticlimactic."

Her words echoed in the small space. Trying to turn the knife brought no change, and her attempt to move the weapon in any direction other than in and out met with the same result.

"Fine. Be that way." She took a deep breath and shunted magic into the blade, willing it to reveal whatever secrets it held. A click sounded, and a portion of the wall about a foot to the left of the dagger swung inward. She had to crouch and pass through sideways to fit. Fortunately, the passage beyond was short. It ended in a wooden door, one far less rough than anything she'd seen thus far in the village. It opened on well-preserved hinges as she pushed through. Behind it lay a room that immediately reminded her of her parents' bunker in New Orleans.

A lamp overhead came to life as she entered and a soft glow emanated from it to banish the room's shadows. It was rectangular, longer than it was wide, and the two side walls had long tables running down them. Again, they were wood and of a craftsmanship that exceeded the village outside. *So my parents probably brought them here by portal.* The far wall held three floor-to-ceiling wooden cabinets, each with closed double doors.

Wooden storage boxes rested on about half the table area and the remainder of the space was empty except for the sheen of dust that covered all the horizontal surfaces in the room. Two uncomfortable-looking chairs were tucked under the table to the right. She lifted the lid of the closest box and set it aside. Within the container was a jumble of books and papers. She examined a few but they were written in the language of House Leblanc that she hadn't yet had time to learn. With a sigh, she returned them and covered the crate again.

She checked a few more but discovered nothing that brought either information or clarity. *I'll have to take these to Emalia. She can add them to her to-do list.* The thought of her great-aunt inspired a smile. Her efforts in New Atlantis agreed with her, and she seemed more alive with each day that passed. It made pushing so much work on her almost guilt-free. *Almost.*

When she was no longer able to distract herself by checking the less interesting items, she approached the cabinets at the rear of the room. They were identical in every way, and the tables ended far enough from them that the doors could swing open unhindered. She opened the one on the left and was surprised to find it empty. The hangars and shelves reminded her of the locker in her parents' other secret hideaway, and she assumed they might have once stored the uniforms and associated equipment there.

She checked the one on the far right next. Four black backpacks, each filled to bursting, rested on shelves. She pulled one out and almost dropped it on her foot due to the unexpected weight. It unzipped to reveal a treasure trove of emergency supplies, from packets of dried food to first aid items.

So, my parents had go-bags for us. That was smart and they are something I need to move back to Earth. Being able to portal from danger made the gear less necessary than it might be for someone without that ability, but preparation was always good. She hauled out the other three and lugged all of them into the center of the room.

Finally, she couldn't delay it any longer. She strode to the remaining cabinet and yanked the doors open. Inside, carefully mounted in what could only be custom holders, was an assortment of more weapons than she'd ever seen in a single place other than Alessand's shop. The doors and the sides held smaller ones like knives for cutting, stabbing, and throwing. One with a missing partner looked exactly like the dagger she'd used to open the room, and she tucked it into her belt.

The back wall had a clear dividing line about two-thirds of the way up. Above were four pairs of pistols and two rifles. Below were swords, two sized for larger people and two for smaller. Unlike the elegant weapon she attempted to reconstruct, these were basic items designed for efficiency. The leather-wrapped handles looked well worn.

She sat quickly, even though she hadn't made the conscious decision to do so. The reality that her parents had fought and probably killed criminals outside the law could no longer be ignored. She'd chatted to Tanyith about his girlfriend's belief that they were vigilantes. Perhaps, by definition, that's what her parents had been. But so were she, Tanyith, and the others who fought for what they believed was right. She wouldn't think less of them because of it.

Cali pushed herself to her feet, suddenly filled with directionless anger. "No, it's more than that. They should be thanked—or celebrated—for doing what others couldn't. Maybe there were mistakes and maybe there weren't. But if good people do nothing, evil flourishes. And, like them, I have only four words to say to that. Not. On. My. Watch."

She grabbed a backpack and emptied it, then dumped the smaller weapons, including the pistols, into it. She hefted it over her shoulder and took one last look around her. It wasn't all she'd hoped for unless important secrets lay inside the crates but it was enough.

Now, it's time to see if Tanyith wants new daggers. With a smile, she headed to the exit.

A night's sleep had tempered the enthusiasm she'd felt at the discovery of her parents' weapon stash. A vague sense of exhaustion pressed at her—not a physical tiredness but a mental one. Her life had too many open loops at the moment, and the way her subconscious constantly poked and prodded at them was like picking scabs only to discover the wound beneath hadn't closed.

"But, on the good side, I'm smart enough to know that going to the bunker alone was stupid and I won't make that mistake again." Fyre wore the same disapproving expression he'd had since she'd told him he couldn't join her. He sat stiffly in the corner of the apartment's living room and watched as she prepared a bowl of cereal for breakfast in the small attached kitchen.

She took an apple out of the basket on the counter and threw it at him. He snapped it out of the air and chomped noisily three times, then swallowed with a gulp. It didn't make him appear any less annoyed at her.

Cali sighed. "Look, I'm sorry. Can we let it go, please? I

promise, we're together from now on." His expression remained unchanged but the emotions that radiated from him softened. "If I give you another apple, will you quit it?"

"I can get my own apples," he muttered.

With a laugh, she threw a second one at him and he caught it with a loud crunch. "Yeah, I know you can but at heart, you like to play as much as the rest of us." She pulled the refrigerator open, checked the date on the milk, and put the bowl of Honey Nut Cheerios on the shelf beside it. "I think the milk is old enough that it may have achieved consciousness. Let's have breakfast in New Atlantis instead."

After the anticipated meal—which consisted of Emalia's always amazing sourdough French toast—Cali and Fyre cleared the Oriceran bunker and moved everything into one of the spare rooms in the mansion. She portaled to the tavern in time to pick up Scoppic and Invel and brought them to work with Emalia.

Well, Scoppic is here to research, anyway. The way the Drow and her great-aunt lit up when they saw each other was a clear indication that Invel had interests beyond the collection of books and papers scattered around the formal dining room table.

She left them to their tasks with a wave and a parting, "Find out everything you can. I need every last piece of information you can get out of there. None of you will leave that room until every word is translated." The responses varied but all were notably disrespectful. She looked at Fyre and shook her head. "Honestly. I'm the matriarch of a noble house and people still treat me like a slacker."

The Draksa grinned at her. "Well, you did withdraw from your classes so you are kind of slacking."

"Ya gotta rub salt in the wound, don't ya, buddy? You are not a nice draggylizard." She'd discovered the name she'd made up annoyed him and since then, had done her best to include it in conversation whenever possible. "Besides, I do have a few things on my plate at the moment. My career as an investigator will have to wait a while."

Maybe forever, at this rate. My future is certainly turning out different than I'd expected.

Cali took the winding path to the chamber where her parents' memories were stored. Fyre entered with her, looked around the room as if impressed, and slipped under the large wingback chair. With both of them in the space, even with most of him hidden under her, claustrophobia crept in at the edges of her mind. She banished those feelings with an act of will and did the same with the many concerns that banged around in her head. None of them was relevant in that moment as she was there to ask a difficult question. The answer wouldn't change how she felt about her parents but it nonetheless carried a palpable weight.

Now focused, she selected the last of the rods in the sequence, which she and Emalia had agreed was likely the final one recorded. She slotted it into the basin and an illusion of her mother, frozen in time, flowed into existence above it. In silence, she absorbed the finer details of the image, the kind face, and the long dark hair. Finally, her heart full of longing for what could have been, she managed to croak, "Hi, Mom."

The magical representation suddenly came to life and her mother's face softened in a wide smile. "Cali, my love. It's good to see you."

"And you, Mom. I don't know if I've ever said thank you for leaving these memories for me. So, thank you."

Her mother nodded. "It was the least we could do when we discovered we would be forced to leave all the safety nets we'd constructed for you and your brother behind."

A lump of emotion caught in her chest and she coughed to banish it. "So…uh, I have a question for you. Well, a couple. The first is, when did you record this? It's the last one in the cabinet so I've assumed it's the final message."

"I created this on the day before we intended to leave New Atlantis. Well, in the early, early morning of the day we intended to depart. If it's the last one, I can only presume we made it out as we hoped."

"Why didn't you make any more in New Orleans?" She hadn't planned to ask that question but the words leapt out of her mouth before she knew they were coming.

Her mother gave her a soft smile. "I can't say what happened after this moment, but I can tell you we wanted to. It might be that we couldn't find the magical materials needed as they are unique to New Atlantis as far as we knew. Or…it could be anything, really. We had hoped to continue to leave these for you both until you were grown." Her expression stretched into a grin. "At least that's what I said to your father. Personally, I wanted to keep doing it forever."

Cali laughed. "It was a good plan. But if you did it, I

haven't been able to find it. Although that's not why I came. There's something else I need to know."

Her mother's face turned somber. "I will share whatever I can, of course."

"A friend who visited a secret place you left on the surface thinks that you and Dad were vigilantes who hunted and killed criminals outside the law. She doesn't argue that the people you apparently targeted mostly deserved what they got." Even talking to a magical version of her parent, she felt the need to soften the accusation. "But her opinion is that it was wrong. I don't agree with her but what I want to know is if you had planned something like that. Or, if you didn't, if you think it might be something you'd do."

The other woman's lips curled and she frowned as she considered the question in silence. It stretched long enough that Cali started to fear she'd somehow broken whatever made the conversations with the past versions of her parents possible.

Finally, her mother sighed. "We were angry when I recorded this. Very angry. At the general indifference of most of the Nine and the betrayals by the others. But I can't imagine a situation where we would do such a thing of our own volition."

Her heart started to beat with its normal rhythm again as the woman continued to speak. "We intended to go to the surface and live anonymously until you were old enough to choose whether to join us or not in an effort to reclaim our lives and standing in New Atlantis. During that time, we had only three goals—survival, raising you, and finding a way to save your brother.

Whatever we did should have been driven by one of those.

"Anything is possible, of course." Her mother shrugged. "But I don't think it's likely that we would have picked a fight with anyone or that we would have engaged in one we could have avoided. I can't say what might have changed after we left the city for the dirt above, but I cannot conceive of us suddenly becoming crusaders without a very, very powerful reason."

She sighed as relief surged through her. "Good. That's good." The emotions from Fyre, which had supported her through the whole conversation, were in agreement. "Thank you. I knew it had to be something other than what Barton thought."

The magical image nodded. "Keep an open mind, my daughter. There's no telling what might have happened. But I'm glad you've found comfort in my answer."

Cali stood and held the rod for a moment. "Thanks, Mom. I miss you." She pulled the slim wand free and stored it in its receptacle, then knuckled the tears away from the corners of her eyes. With a sniff, she gave a hoarse command, "Let's go, scale-face. We have important things to do."

When they arrived in the dining room, Emalia, Invel, and Scoppic were all bent over the table. The gnome had to stand on a chair to manage it. One of the boxes she'd retrieved from the Oriceran bunker stood open on its surface and papers were spread out. Her great-aunt looked up as she entered. "Cali, good. Come here."

She obeyed and peered at the object of their interest. It was a plain sheet of legal pad paper with writing on it in her mother's hand. "What does it say?"

"It gives the location of another piece of the sword," Invel replied. "One of the other families apparently shared it to taunt your parents, or at least that's what Elisinia wrote."

Cali frowned. "How does providing them the location accomplish that?"

Emalia shook her head. "Because it's virtually unreachable."

"How so?"

Scoppic adjusted his glasses as he straightened on the chair to meet her eyes. "You see, it was given as a gift to a very bad person to celebrate his ascension to a new role. The blade fragment is hidden inside a golden statue of a tiger."

They all stared expectantly at her, which made her feel like she was missing something important from the conversation. "Okay, so, let me ask a different way. What the hell are you talking about?"

The older woman chuckled. "According to your mother, the statue was given to Peng Jian, the leader of a criminal organization in Shenyang, China. She writes that the group's leadership and much of its membership is made up of former elite soldiers. Since his personal icon is the tiger, there is no way he'll surrender a gift of such significance willingly."

Her brain whipped through the information again and

immediately began to spit out possibilities. Each was more ludicrous than the last. After a few moments of that, she shrugged. "Well, then. If that's where it is, that's where I'll go." Fyre growled, and she uttered a chagrined laugh. "Correction, that's where we'll go."

She sighed and shook her head as the only reasonable path forward swam into clarity. "I'll owe so many people too many favors after this."

CHAPTER TEN

Tanyith portaled to the docks of New Atlantis and within minutes, was already annoyed at being in the domed city. It wasn't the location itself, of course. The architecture was pleasant and most of the people were gregarious and welcoming. No, the reason he was there was what soured his mood. Finding a note on his door to summon him to a meeting with the bastards who threatened those he cared for would always put him in a belligerent frame of mind.

He hired one of the runners who constantly hung around the docks and sent the girl with a message for Cali —simply to tell her he was in town and going to visit "old friends." She'd know what it meant and if he ran into trouble and didn't report in after a reasonable amount of time, he imagined she'd come looking for him. At least, he hoped so.

The walk to the Privateer Pub was shorter than it had been from the Leblanc mansion and decidedly more pleasant to do on his own rather than in the company of the goon who had escorted him on the previous occasion. The weather under the dome was warm and comfortable, the same as it always was. He thought with a small laugh that if New Orleans could find a way to accomplish the same thing, it would become the prime tourist destination in the country.

The afternoon crowd inside the venue was stunningly normal, merely folks having lunch and drinks in the same way as they might anywhere. It was easy to forget, amongst the battles and the politics and the people trying to manipulate him, that New Atlantis was mostly full of ordinary citizens. Admittedly, they were of a higher economic class than him but that didn't make them any more special.

Rather than turn toward the back room where those who had rudely demanded his presence would doubtless be waiting, he veered left and headed to the bar. The bartender was different than the one who had been on the job the last time. He was a strong-looking middle-aged man who had let some of his former muscle go to fat but was still demonstrably imposing enough to keep his clientele in line. A large black mustache drew attention away from the rest of his face very effectively. "What'll ya have?"

"A pint of whatever you've got in the cask." He grinned and gestured toward the small barrel.

"Good choice. It's strong, though. You'll want to take it slow." The liquid that filled the glass as he twisted the valve was deep-red and ended with a crimson-tinted white foam. Tanyith accepted the drink, took a sip, and nodded in appreciation.

"Nice. Thanks." He threw some local currency on the

bar, double what his beverage cost. "Can I ask you a question?"

The man scooped the offering up and replied, "Sure. I won't promise to answer, though."

"I'm meeting with the folks in the back room but I don't know them very well. They're from the Malniet family but outside the main line, I think. Is there anything else you can tell me?"

With a guarded look at the back door, the bartender leaned closer. "I can tell you three things. First, you're right, although they're fairly close to the main line, regardless of blood. They're often the voice of the patriarch in this part of town. Second, they have their hands in all kinds of things around here." The way he said it strongly suggested that he referred to criminal activities. "And, finally, you don't want to cross 'em. People who do tend to wind up disappearing—probably as shark food." He straightened and moved to the other end of the bar without waiting for a reply.

Great. Well, it's not any worse than I expected but certainly not as good as I might have hoped. He drank half the glass at a relaxed pace, perfectly fine with making them wait a little longer before he strolled to the back. The door yielded to his push and he passed through to find the scene essentially as he'd anticipated.

The two sat in the same positions they'd occupied the last time—the pocked-face man on the left and the freckled blonde on the right. He took the chair across from them and spun it so he could sit reversed and lean his arms on the top. "It's so great to see you again. Thanks so much for the invitation."

The man laughed. "Hardly an invitation, but if it makes you feel better to call it that, you do what you need to do."

He answered the taunt with a smile. "Oh, I very much doubt you'd enjoy it if I did what I need to do."

The woman shook her head. "Let's not lose focus, gentlemen. Tanyith, don't forget that your lady friends are one word away from taking their last breath. And if you have any doubt about our resolve in that area, feel free to test us. We can give up one without any particular damage to our plans. Which would you like to see die first? The old girlfriend or the new?"

He suppressed a growl at her words but allowed the anger to show on his face. Barton had eyes watching Sienna and was naturally wary in her own right, but magic tilted the balance. It was always possible that the Malniets could make good on the threat against one or the other. "Fine. You've made your point. What do you want?"

The man rested his elbows on the table and steepled his fingers. "Oh, several things. You won't want to do them but in the end, I'm sure you'll realize that you need to."

Yeah, that would probably be true if your compulsion was still working. Since you're not freaking out right now, I guess Nylotte managed to hide the evidence of her efforts. "Anything's possible. Can we quit dancing and get to the point? I have places to be."

The woman grinned and snarked, "Are you going to visit Leblanc? Maybe add her to your little harem? I think the Jehenel idiot might have gotten there first."

Tanyith stared at her for a moment, his face expressionless but his eyes smoldering, and turned his attention to her compatriot. "You should put a muzzle on her. She brings your collective IQ way down and it's fairly low to begin with."

The man tilted his head mockingly. "And yet you're the one on our hook rather than the other way around. What does that say about you, lover boy?" He leaned forward and lowered his hands. "Okay, enough fun. You'll do three things for us. First, you'll put the torch to that wench Usha's place. It doesn't matter if anyone's in it or not but if it's still standing in a week, we'll move on to the endgame of our little relationship."

His eyes widened. "You're picking up some powerful enemies, aren't you? One would have thought that House Malniet had enough on its plate right now."

The other man didn't respond to his taunt. "Second, you'll collect information on your city's council of idiots—where they live, where they work, and who they love. Your connection to the dwarf should make that easy for you."

The hell I will. He shook his head. "That's asking too much."

"Like most things in this partnership we have going on here, such decisions aren't your call. You'll do it or you'll face the consequences of not doing it. And we haven't reached the best part yet."

He could see in the way the woman tensed that the moment Nylotte had warned him about wasn't far away. The Drow had said that the caster would probably try to use the spell while he was in front of them to ensure it was still working. They'd determined together that it would likely be some form of discomfort and that the only way to deal with it was to fake it when it happened. The back of his mind began to chart angles and distances for the battle that would follow if he failed.

The man grinned broadly and seemed almost gleeful. "Finally, you'll go down off the bat when the Leblanc girl calls upon you to fight our house. Our relatives will know not to kill you, and you'll simply let them hit you and take you out of the combat."

Tanyith laughed. He couldn't help it. As he started to reply, he felt the surge from the woman. Stiffening, he twisted like his back—which had been the most frequent source of pain while he was under the influence of her magic—had cramped. He mimed holding in a shout before he slowly returned to normal. When he thought enough time had passed to sell the act, he said, "How do I know your people will keep your word?"

"You don't." The man shrugged. "But why would we throw such a useful tool away? You've given us everything we've wanted from you so far and that's led to some very interesting discoveries about chemicals that affect magicals. We can put that into use in oh so many ways. So, no, we don't intend to lose your services yet."

Deliberately, he scowled, although the sentiment behind the pretense was real enough that he could react the way they most likely expected him to. "When I get out from under this, you're dead."

His contact laughed. "The only way you'll get out from under anything is if you're dead. I'm not worried. But by all means, fight and see what it gets you. Hell, to be honest, I kind of want you to."

He pushed to his feet and threw his chair aside to clatter on the floor. Neither of his blackmailers rose to the provocation, and he stalked through the door and slammed it shut behind him. People in the restaurant area turned to stare at him, but he ignored them and hurried out of the bar. The fresh air helped to calm him, as only part of his actions and reactions had been false.

I can't wait until I can beat the arrogance off their faces.

He had cooled off completely by the time he reached the Leblanc grounds and Invel opened the front door to let him in. "Caliste is sleeping," the Drow explained, "and Emalia and Scoppic are translating. That left Jenkins and I, and he's not the best at physical tasks, from what I understand."

The disembodied caretaker of the house replied calmly, "Indeed so. Fortunately, there are so many around to help now." He sounded pleased and Tanyith imagined that if he'd been stuck alone in an abandoned home for as long as the retainer had, he would feel the same way.

Invel gestured toward the kitchen. "There's coffee if you like or hot water for tea. Plus various snacks. We'll have an afternoon break in an hour or so if you'll join us." He nodded and followed him into the kitchen. They chatted amiably and were eventually joined by Emalia, who bustled around organizing sandwiches and snack cakes while the Dark Elf made several pots of tea.

By the time it was all ready, Scoppic, Cali, and Fyre had also arrived. She looked a little worn but had an air of resolve about her that hadn't been there when they'd last been together. "What's going on?" he asked.

She shrugged. "Emalia, Scoppic, and Invel found the next shard."

"And?"

"It'll be a little hard to get." The others laughed with varying degrees of disbelief. "Okay, it'll be very hard to get."

Tanyith grinned. "Being your friend is never boring."

"Just wait." She shook her head. "You don't know the half of it. But at least it comes with fringe benefits like the constant risk of death."

He nodded. "Well, who could ask for anything more?"

CHAPTER ELEVEN

Cali had sent Tanyith to the tavern and he had portaled from there to his apartment to get ready. He and Kendra had been unable to find much time to spend together of late since the situation with the Atlanteans and the Zatoras had landed squarely in the lap of her inter-agency task force.

But tonight, they'd both agreed to set aside whatever they had going on to go out on a date. He had made a reservation at one of New Orleans' trendiest restaurants and had plans to see a blues band at a dive bar thereafter. In his opinion, fancy meals and local bands were the best things the city had to offer.

On the side of the Quarter that was closest to the Drunken Dragons, Effervescence was small, beautiful, and difficult to get into. He'd had to put down a hefty deposit simply to reserve two seats at the bar as their tables were booked months in advance. They'd be expected to have drinks, the obligatory bottle of champagne, and a tasting menu chosen by the chef.

It was one of his favorite ways to spend an evening. They would face no decisions other than what to drink and he had the opportunity to focus all his attention on his companion. He finished dressing, put cufflinks in his shirt, and pulled his suit jacket on before he portaled to an alley near the restaurant.

After the short walk to his destination, he realized he'd arrived before Kendra and stood outside the clean white building with its black shutters and ornate ebony doors to wait. He watched the passersby warily, alert for trouble, but the people on the street were merely normal folks living normal lives as far as he could tell.

Tanyith couldn't remember having lived a normal life. The events since his imprisonment had banished all of that from his memory and he didn't see any likely change in that situation anytime soon. He was determined to enjoy each moment for what it was, to flow like a river from one set of rapids to the next, and to seek calm when not among the rocks.

The sight of his date made him smile. Kendra Barton wore a dress, which was as unusual as anything else in his life. It was black and thin straps over her shoulders supported a form-fitting sheath that ended above her knees. She carried a clutch purse that he was sure would be adequate to hold a pistol and probably a set of handcuffs. Her hair held more of a wave than usual, and her makeup was more pronounced. He strode forward to intercept her and kissed her cheek in greeting. "Hello, gorgeous."

She stepped back and made a show of studying him carefully. "Hello yourself. Not bad, Shale. If you don't ruin things with your mouth, I might invite you home later."

"It's always my mouth that betrays me," he said with a laugh.

"That's the case with most criminals."

"We're back to that, are we?" He raised an eyebrow.

The detective broke into a grin. "Nah, I'm only screwing with you. So, this is the place, huh?"

He nodded, opened the door for her, and gazed appreciatively at the view as she preceded him into the restaurant. "We're at the bar," he said, and she moved to the nearest seats with reserved placards on them. He slid onto the chair next to hers, and the bartender appeared a moment later.

She was a thin woman, blonde and probably in her mid-forties, wearing an immaculate black dress that covered her from neck to wrists and disappeared behind the bar. Her metal bangle bracelets chimed against one another as she smiled and asked, "What can I get you two?" She slid wooden coasters in front of them.

Kendra said, "Manhattan," and Tanyith held up two fingers. The bartender bustled away and he grinned at his date.

"So. How ya been?"

"Fine, except for the storm of garbage that came from what went down at the Zatora place."

He nodded. "Yeah. I can see how that would be a challenge for y'all. Did you find out anything interesting?"

She accepted her drink from the bartender's hands and took a sip before she set it down carefully and looked at him with what he thought of as her cop eyes—sharp, inquisitive, and suspicious. "Signs of a fight that included magic. You wouldn't know about that, would you?"

"Maybe, maybe not." He shrugged. "It'll cost you to find out." One of the difficult parts of their relationship was that they often had to keep secrets from each other for personal or professional reasons. The only thing they could agree to commit to as an absolute was sharing if safety was an issue. As the action at the mansion didn't qualify as that, he wouldn't betray Cali's confidence without a significant quid pro quo.

She laughed, unoffended. "Nah, it's not worth the price right now, whatever it is. I don't have anything to offer."

His entendre-laden reply was forestalled by the arrival of their first dish. Oysters, of course, one of the key gastronomic elements of New Orleans Cuisine. These had been grilled and were dotted with brown gravy. He used the tiny fork provided to spear one from its shell and eat it. He wouldn't have expected a chipotle sauce with the seafood but it worked well. Kendra lifted the shell to her mouth and ate the meat that way, and he momentarily lost his train of thought. She noticed and laughed at him again.

"Ah, Shale, you're so easy sometimes." She offered him the third but he declined, and she snagged that one with the fork. "Delicious. So, what's going on that you are willing to talk about, then?"

"Oh, the usual. Upcoming battles, the threat of you and Sienna getting killed, and damn Aiden Walsh is out there somewhere causing trouble." He'd shared the knowledge that Walsh was part of the Zatoras but nothing else from the battle.

"Convince those blackmailing bastards to visit the city. I'll lock 'em up."

He chuckled. "Did you get an AET team while I wasn't

looking?" The anti-magic version of SWAT wasn't a resource available to the NOPD as far as he knew.

She shook her head. "No such luck. But I'm confident we can take them." She lowered her voice. "We found a cache of anti-magic bullets in the mansion. Each member of the task force has a magazine full. It's not nearly enough but it's a step in the right direction, for sure."

The next course arrived, some kind of dumpling with a soy sauce and he bit into it carefully to discover that it was filled with sausage—hot, spicy, and delicious. He yanked the napkin from his lap to his mouth to avoid dribbling juice onto his suit. Kendra managed her portion with far more elegance.

Suddenly, an internal pressure he hadn't noticed suddenly gained impetus and he had to speak. "Hey. Can I be serious with you for a minute?"

She dabbed her red-painted lips and nodded. "Sure. Shoot."

"I need more."

His companion chuckled, low and sultry. "Is that an invitation? Or are you referring to the food?"

He shook his head and tried to calm the hammering of his heart. "No. I mean that I want to…uh, move our relationship forward, I suppose."

She laughed again, this time a little more playfully. "Are you asking me to go steady?"

That inspired a reciprocal laugh from him. "Yeah. I guess I kind of am. Or we could always do the grown-up version and move in together."

Her expression morphed slowly into something entirely more serious. "You're not joking, right?"

"No. Not even slightly."

"You actually want to live with me."

Tanyith nodded. "Look, I don't know what the future holds but spending what few uncommitted minutes we have apart from one another doesn't make sense to me. On my part, at least." He didn't add the words but his mind supplied them. *Unless you don't feel the same way, that is, in which case, I'll find a hole to hide in for a decade or so.*

Her reply was delayed by the arrival of the next course. She filled her mouth with the miniature quiche and chewed slowly while he did the same and wondered how long she'd make him wait for her answer. Finally, she finished the mouthful, drained her drink, and turned to him with a smile on her face. "Okay."

Relief coursed through him. "Really?"

"Really really. However, we'll need to set some ground rules."

"That seems fair. You go first."

"No criminal activity of any kind in my apartment. No contraband, no illegal weapons, and nothing that could cause me to lose my job."

He raised an eyebrow. "Oh, it'll be your apartment, will it?"

Kendra laughed. "We both know your apartment is a hole compared to mine."

"Okay. Fair enough. Now I have one. No peeking at one another's phones."

She imitated his eyebrow-raise. "Already planning to step out on me, are you?"

He shook his head. "No. But we both need to protect

confidential information and I can't see any other way to ensure that."

"Agreed."

The bartender interrupted to uncork a bottle of pink champagne and pour them each a glass, which signaled that the more substantial courses of their meal would soon arrive. Kendra added, "No extra expectations. We live together but we still do our own things. When we're in the same place at the same time, it's all good, but no demands. I can't deal with that right now."

Tanyith lifted his glass in a toast. "Me neither. So, to togetherness."

She tapped hers against his with a small clink. "Togetherness."

They spent the rest of the meal in happy conversation and added one or two details to the arrangement as they occurred to them. When it was over, they strolled down the street to where the car she had called would pick them up. Even at night and even this far on the fringes of the Quarter, a fair number of folks wandered around. He nodded at a man who strolled past them. "Do you think they know what's going on? Do they realize there's a gang war happening right under their noses?"

The detective shook her head. "I doubt it. And that's probably for the best. Most people can't face that kind of stress day in and day out and they shouldn't have to. That's where those like us come in."

He laughed. "Idiots, you mean."

"You said it, not me. But what I meant was the fighters. Most people are maxed-out fighting their own battles.

Some of us can give more, though, and we're called to do it. It's in our nature."

"That's an awful nice dress for a fighter, by the way." He grinned.

She responded with a smirk. "You should see what's under it."

"I'd like that. I'd like that very much."

A Honda Accord pulled up, the one the ride app on her phone had promised. "Well then, get in and do something about that at our apartment."

CHAPTER TWELVE

The day had arrived. Rion Grisham hadn't slept at all the night before and spent it instead in the company of a bottle of Jack Daniels and his memories—not only of Colin Todd, although those were not far from his mind, but of the path that had brought him to this place. From the early days as a leg-breaker for organized crime in the north to his current position, it had been a fairly straight diagonal and he'd always traveled upward toward more wealth and power.

Lately, though, that arrow had become a flat line because of the actions of the magicals in his city. He didn't consider himself a xenophobe and would happily work with or take from any race, color, creed, or species if it moved him closer to the things he wanted. The Atlantean gang was another matter entirely, however. It had been foolish to think that keeping them around would spread the heat from the authorities enough to make that strategy worthwhile. It wasn't often he did something so ultimately wrong-headed, and he couldn't imagine why he'd done it on this occasion. But after they'd seen his former lieutenant off with the proper pomp and circumstance, it would be time to set that error to rights.

With a groan, he levered himself up from the table, ran a hand through his rumpled hair, and padded toward the shower to scald the sleep away. Only a half-hour remained before the start of the day's events and he owed it to Colin to be at his best.

When Strang and Ozahl arrived, he was suitably prepared to face the day. He'd shaved, tamed the tangle atop his head, and dressed all in black—shoes, suit, shirt, and tie. The clothes were cut to obscure the presence of the guns under each armpit and the one at his lower back. Each was filled with anti-magic rounds, and he carried a spare mag for all three in his pockets. When the enemy came—and he had no doubt they would—he'd be ready.

The point of this meeting was to make sure the rest of his people would be ready as well. He gestured at the table and his lieutenants took their places while he rang the bottom floor to demand coffee and breakfast. Assured that it was on its way, he sat and looked at his two companions. "So. Today's the day."

Strang nodded. "It's gonna be a perfect one with a good temperature, and it's sunny. We'll have the right kind of sendoff."

The mage showed signs of agitation, shifted in his seat, and drummed his fingers. *That's not much of a surprise. When things get tough, you start to fray around the edges. Some fierce magical you are.* Grisham stared at him and asked, "Is there a problem?"

In response, the man sighed and straightened. "You know this is a bad idea. Why are you going through with it? The dead don't care. They're already gone."

He shook his head. "We've been through this. It's not about Colin. It's about the rest of my people. We have to show them we're not afraid."

The magical looked as average as he always did, with mousy-brown unstyled hair, khakis, and a button-down shirt. No one would ever imagine that he could be a threat, which was probably exactly what he wanted. Ozahl leaned forward and spoke in a low, sharp tone. "But we should be afraid. This is a security nightmare. Hell, for all we know, the entire church is already wired to explode."

The Zatora leader chuckled dismissively. "You worry too much. We've had people watching the cathedral for days, inside and out. No one's done anything of the kind. We planned for this, remember? We're ready."

The mage shook his head and muttered something under his breath, but he leaned back in his chair, apparently content to still his protests for the moment, at least. Breakfast arrived on a rolling cart, and they busied themselves for a few minutes spreading toast with butter, preparing cups of chicory coffee, and loading their plates with eggs and potatoes. They ate in silence and the unspoken agreement that fuel was a priority momentarily delayed the conversation.

When he had finished eating, Grisham tossed his napkin onto the table. "Okay, Jack, what's the plan?"

Strang set his silverware aside and downed his coffee.

The man had put a dark suit on over a dark shirt and as usual, it all looked too small on him. His shave was smooth, though, both on his face and his head. "We already have lookouts in every direction. Four teams of two on the roof, at least one on each street for three blocks, and two guards posted at each entrance. We swept the location two nights ago and again last night. It'll be done hourly today."

His boss nodded. "What are they carrying?"

"Everything we could find. Pistols everywhere, plus rifles or shotguns for those not in public places. The shooters on the roof have their weapon of choice, and their spotters have ARs."

"Anti-magic bullets?" Ozahl asked,

The other lieutenant shrugged. "Some. We don't have the right caliber for the snipers and I've never heard of shotgun rounds of that kind. But more than half our people have at least one magazine."

Grisham nodded. "It'll have to do. So, Ozahl, what have you done to prepare?"

The mage straightened again, having slouched in his chair to finish his coffee. "Last night, I did the wards inside the building. We should be warned if someone uses magic to get in. As we discussed, doing it earlier would have tipped our hand but I decided that since the place was locked down, it wouldn't be a risk." The leader grunted, and he continued. "I'll be on the roof too and will be able to detect others' magic. I'm better than any other magical in this city, anyway, so I should be able to identify anyone who tries to sneak in under an illusion."

He turned to look at Strang. "I'll want someone with me who can protect me from attack and be my communication person. Two, if we have them to spare. Be sure they have extra anti-magic ammunition. I'll be a prime target."

That drew a frown from the man. "But I thought you were better than everyone. Why do you need protection?" The minuscule quantity of positive feelings the two might have felt for one another in the past had clearly been banished by recent events.

The magical gave a thin smile. "It doesn't matter how good I am if the Atlanteans portal a group of folks up there to kill me. I could survive and escape, of course, but you, your people, and our boss would all be sitting ducks. Of course, if that's what you want, I'm game."

Strang growled annoyance. "You'll have your guards."

Grisham nodded. "Excellent. It sounds like we're ready. Now, let's go over everything again from the start. Jack, tell me where the outer cordon is positioned."

Across town in the main room of the Shark Nightclub, Usha sat on the low stage and stared at her audience of one. Danna was seated at a front table in her fighting clothes—tough black leather pants, matching boots that reached past her calves, and a bright red leather jacket. She felt underdressed in her jeans and sweatshirt but she wasn't willing to put her battle dress on until the last minute.

"So. What's the plan?" her second in command asked.

She grinned. "What makes you think I have one? I thought we'd simply roll in and cause trouble."

The woman laughed. "Please. The Champion of New Atlantis doesn't 'simply roll in.'"

"Dammit. Betrayed by my awesomeness." She shook her head and her long ropes of hair swatted her cheeks. "What do you think we should do?"

"Well, answer me this. Is the funeral part of the reason you activated the magic in the drugs?"

Usha stiffened in surprise. "How do you know about that?"

"I hear many things." Her companion shrugged. "I keep my ear to the streets as you know. Plus, I've still made deliveries. If enough people say they're feeling off, you start to put two and two together. Maybe the better question is why you chose to not tell me." It was delivered without any particular venom but it nonetheless hurt to hear it.

"I didn't want you tainted by my choice. Or anyone else, for that matter. It was my decision to make and I made it."

Danna nodded. "Sometimes, you should try not being an island."

Usha laughed. "Like you're one to talk. I still don't know about your mystery man and that would be far more fun to share. We all have our secrets."

The teasing reference pulled a smile from her second. "Touché. So, is it part of today?"

She nodded. "When the rest of our people get here in an hour or so, we'll take anyone who won't be useful in a fight and get them out on the streets. They'll spread the word that Grisham and his people are responsible for the withdrawal symptoms they think they feel. Between that and the way the magic fires them up, by the time the funeral starts at sunset, everyone who's been taking Shine will be primed and ready to kill any Zatora they see."

"And the magicals?"

Her shrug was dismissive. "I couldn't be sure the council would refrain from interfering with our plans and bringing their individual communities to bear. So, with their magics weakened for a time, the Zarcanum-using magicals in the city won't be able to play much of a role even if the do-gooders at the top call upon them to do so."

Danna shook her head. "It seems like you have that part well-covered. What about the rest of it?"

Usha stood, began to pace the room, and gestured as she talked. "My first thought was to trap the venue or to get our people inside and have them wait. But we saw Zatora presence way earlier than expected, so that option wasn't viable."

"So they know we're coming."

"I'm not sure know is the right word. At the same time, it would be foolish to think we wouldn't and they're not that stupid. Certainly, if the positions were reversed, they'd do the same. While there's no way they could be aware that we were behind the whole thing from the start, it's also safe to assume we'd take advantage of it. They'll underestimate our commitment, though. At least that's what I'm hoping."

Her second in command nodded, crossed her legs, and bounced her foot in time with Usha's steps as they echoed through the space. "How committed are we?"

Usha grinned. "We're all in. Every person. We'll get Grisham tonight or we'll die trying."

The other woman whistled dramatically. "Damn, girl, you're fired up."

She laughed. "I've had enough, Danna. It's not that I'm tired because actually, I'm more energized than I've been in ages. It's simply that I'm sick of it all. The Zatoras, the pretentious magicals and their ineffective council, the smaller gangs and independents who bite around the edges of our territory because we can't spare the attention from the big fish to deal with the minnows. And, of course, the nonsense with Caliste Leblanc." She shook her head and anger rose with every word. "After tonight, everything will be different. And once we start down this road, we don't stop until we win."

Danna rose to her feet and turned slowly to keep her gaze locked on her boss. "And what constitutes winning?" Her voice was a mixture of excitement and concern but definitely held more of the former.

"For tonight? Grisham and his top people dead and the rest run off. After that, we'll deal with everything else, one thing after the next, with overwhelming force."

Her second grinned. "It's been a long time since I've seen you like this. It suits you."

"What will suit me is seeing the look on Rion Grisham's face right before the light fades from his eyes and knowing that he knows who beat him. Before the night is out, he'll see that whoever he thought I was, he has no clue about who I really am."

CHAPTER THIRTEEN

Ozahl portaled to the top of the cathedral two hours before the ceremony to begin his preparations. He hadn't remembered that the building had a peaked roof, which rendered his plan to position himself in the middle useless. He chose a side, sat with his back against the low wall that ran along the edge, and wriggled to get comfortable.

He wore his usual illusory persona but had traded in the normal outfit for heavy jeans, boots, and a coat. Beneath it rested a bulletproof vest he'd acquired long before he'd joined Grisham. He wouldn't take any unnecessary chances tonight as for all he knew, the Atlanteans might have found their own source of anti-magic bullets. Plus, there was no guarantee that the Zatoras wouldn't turn on him at an unexpected moment—especially Strang, who seemed to have inherited Colin Todd's innate distrust of him. *Well, that's fine. I killed one of you so there's no reason I can't kill the other.*

Tonight, though, that was Danna's job. Her involvement in the battle made his stomach hurt, but he had no way to keep her out of danger and she wouldn't allow him to if he could. She'd laughed when he'd suggested she sit the fight out—or at least stay in the back—and responded, "I will if you will." He couldn't, of course, so she wouldn't either.

Damn her for being so competent all the time.

With a sigh, he cleared the worries from his mind. He would be required to maintain his focus even more than usual. To say that the magic he planned to perform would be taxing was a serious understatement and he couldn't afford distractions. He nodded to his guards as they finished their climb to the roof and pulled the knotted ropes others had positioned a day before up behind them. "I'll be mostly checked out. If I say anything, relay it. If I need to know something, you'll have to shake me out of my trance or I won't hear you."

They approached and sat on either side of him, removed rifles from over their shoulders, and rested them across their laps. The man on his right replied, "We've got you. You do your thing, we'll do ours." The other one reported in over a walkie talkie to confirm that they were in place.

Ozahl sent his thoughts spiraling inward. When he had blocked out all the sensory input from his body, he sank into his magic and pushed it out slowly. He felt the presence of his guards first, then more people as it spread in a sphere around him. His limit was less than a mile but that would certainly be enough. He didn't want to push beyond the edge of Jackson Square in any case for fear of getting results that weren't aimed at the cathedral itself.

When he found Decatur, identified by the fast-moving people he sensed in cars, he gave his power a new command. Instead of detecting life, he redirected his intention to react to the presence of magic. That would give him a signal if someone used power within the bounds of the spell or if a magical creature such as Leblanc's Draksa partner should appear. Nothing leapt out at him. The greatest challenge for him would be to maintain his discipline until something did because, inevitably, something would. Depending on what triggered his senses, he might even do what he'd promised and provide a warning about it.

If his guards wondered why he suddenly smiled, they didn't interrupt him to find out, which was all for the best.

Inside the cathedral, Grisham made another circuit to ensure that everything Jack Strang had told him was true. With only an hour before the starting time, he wanted a last pass to look for possible trouble locations. Obviously, the biggest one would be the front entrance, where the entire Zatora organization would flood in to attend. It wasn't an optional event because he needed to show everyone in the city of New Orleans that nothing scared him. To do anything else would be to risk losing all they'd spent so much time and effort building up.

"And that won't happen, not while I still draw breath," he muttered under his breath as he nodded to the guards at the side entrance. They'd cleared the basement earlier and locked every access so no one could come from that direction without him knowing about it. The balcony that ran around most of the sanctuary held several of his men and a number of secured ropes so they could descend to the bottom level quickly if needed. All the exits from the main room that led to the rest of the building had been barricaded, and nothing short of explosives would get through them.

If it came down to a melee, his people would win. Those who had it would wear body armor under their funeral clothes and he fully expected knives, blackjacks, and every other kind of street weapon to be near to hand as well. If the enemy tried to use magic from outside, the snipers would eliminate them or his mage would. Ozahl didn't know it, but the two men with him had been tasked with guaranteeing that if anything went wrong, the magical wouldn't make it out of the adventure alive. Tonight, the Zatora leader's trust was limited to himself and maybe Strang.

Grisham finished his circuit and walked to the front of the room where the closed casket rested on a long table, draped in yellow-and-blue cloth. He placed one hand on the top and whispered, "We'll make your death count, my friend. I promise we will."

With thirty minutes to go, things began to happen. Danna crouched atop the building filled with shops that bordered Jackson Square on the side closest to Cafe du Monde and her head moved constantly in all directions. The position gave her a good view of the thickening crowds along Decatur street.

Usha's plan to inflame the drug-using contingent of the citizenry seemed to have paid dividends. The individuals looked as unwell as they were angry. *I'd hoped it wouldn't come to this.* Had she been provided the opportunity, she would have argued against activating the magic. She lacked the brutal dedication that such a sweeping action required. Fortunately or unfortunately, the Atlantean leader had it in excess.

I guess that's what made it possible for her to become Champion. Movement from across the street caught her attention. Members of her gang stalked quietly into position, took seats at the restaurant, watched the buskers who still worked the sidewalks, and posed as tourists. Unlike the sprawling Zatora organization, their group all knew each other. They were fewer in number but stronger in dedication and resolve. Every ounce of that would be needed to bring about the defeat of the enemy.

The square itself became an unofficial gathering point for the crowd, a place for them to talk to each other and reinforce what they already thought—or what Usha had primed them to think—which was that their current pain was the fault of the Zatoras, who right now prepared to gather and honor one of their fallen members. She swiveled to study the cathedral. Hard-looking men and women held position on the entry steps and carefully checked each person who attempted to enter the building. Some received a nod, others required a quiet word, and a few were taken off to the side for what looked like a thorough search.

She unmuted the microphone attached to her earphones and said, "I'd say we have about fifteen minutes before they get up the nerve to start moving. There are Zatora guards in the square but they haven't engaged with the people. They look nervous, though." She raised her eyes to the roof of the cathedral where she knew Ozahl would be and noticed the telltale tip of a rifle barrel. "They have snipers, as expected."

Usha's voice replied in her ears. "Everything is playing out exactly like we thought it would." Danna laughed internally. *Exactly like you thought it would, anyway.* "We'll wait until things start to happen with the humans before we swoop in and engage them."

"That's not particularly surgical," she observed. "It'll be hard to find Grisham in the press."

"Oh, don't worry about that, sweetheart. If we can't find him, we'll go to Plan B."

A shiver of apprehension traced down her spine. The other woman hadn't filled her in on the details of the backup strategy but given how involved and outright violent Plan A was, she feared what else might be on the table. With another glance at the rooftop, she whispered, "Keep safe, love."

Usha was the communication hub for the gang as she wanted to ensure that all commands came from her directly. She hung up with Danna and called each of the men she'd selected to scout the streets around the cathedral. They returned identical reports—there was no sign of additional Zatora reinforcements anywhere nearby. She didn't think Grisham would put all his people into a single kill box but apparently, he was as tired of the status quo as she was.

Before every battle on the path to winning the tournament in New Atlantis, she had finished her preparations in the same way. It seemed only natural that she do so now, as well. She closed her eyes and spread her arms wide.

"Universe, I come to you again with the same promise as always. Win or lose, survive or die, I will not give up. I will not back down. I will not lose my courage. I will be a shining star to rival those in the night sky above the waves and a bright light to illuminate the shimmering currents below them. I swear it with all that I am. Harken to my vow and lend me your grace for the fight ahead."

She opened her eyes again and nodded decisively. Saying the words sounded as right as being back in her combat gear felt. The heavy leather pants that had been patched and resewn after every battle were tucked into her reinforced boots, which had quick-release blades set in the toes and heels. She wore a tight tunic of heavy material cinched at the waist by a wide belt. It held potions, a pair of daggers, and a few tricks. An armored vest similar to what the police used covered her chest and dense ceramic plates protected her upper and lower arms and elbows.

Her hair had been bound and threaded through a ring at the back of the protective collar she wore around her neck. Finally, the hilt of a sword rode over her right shoulder. It was the size of the weapons of the nobility and was similar to the one she'd used in her ascent to Champion.

She was ready and her people were ready. Somewhere,

Rion Grisham thought he was ready too, but he was wrong. It was time to show him how big a mistake he'd made. She pressed the button to contact all her subordinates and snapped the command.

"Go. Go now. No one stops until the Zatoras are no more."

CHAPTER FOURTEEN

Danna chose to deal with the snipers herself so no one else would be up there to present a risk to Ozahl. However, the way they'd been positioned and the unexpected guards she'd seen climb up the side of the cathedral required a change of plan. She'd hoped that she and the mage could simply wait on the roof while the chaos ensued below and then, depending on whose side won, that one could enter at the end to help with the mop-up while the other disappeared.

It had been a good strategy but Grisham's paranoia had screwed it up. Instead of appearing and wiping them out, she summoned invisible force barriers and held them directly between the two sniper positions at the front of the building and the people below. She ducked behind a chimney and only exposed enough of herself to watch the shooters so she could be sure to keep the magic in place.

From her vantage point, she could also see the crowd in Jackson Square begin to move in response to Usha's command. The men they'd seeded among the citizens shouted and pushed as they instigated the kind of virulent response their plans called for. It was like watching the ripples from several stones thrown into a pond as the anger and motion spread. When two ripples met, the speed of those involved increased. In moments, the whole mass of people—probably eighty at least—began to stride toward the entrance to the cathedral.

Across the large green space and in the shadow of the building that ran perpendicular to the church and formed one boundary of the square, figures darted forward but remained low to avoid detection. Usha's plan called for sending the frustrated mob in as a diversion while her people advanced on the periphery. They'd identified the Zatoras' outer defensive layer some time before, and as soon as the group in the middle began to move, the outliers would have been eliminated. Those who watched the other approaches would find their efforts futile. The Atlantean leader had decided to put all her resources in one place and relied on the distraction to keep them safe during their approach.

Shouts emanated from the area of the cathedral stairs as the guards there threatened the oncoming mass of people. That only served to shift them from a fast walk into a run. The sniper rifles barked but the bullets struck the force shields, stopped, and fell, ineffective and unnoticed, to the ground below. Danna pushed more magic into the barriers with a grin at the frustration the shooters doubtless felt. The crowd below flowed out of her line of sight and she knew it would be only moments before blood would begin to spill—which was fine as long as it wasn't hers, Ozahl's, or Usha's.

Only a couple more minutes of this before the fight will move inside, and I can make sure it works out that way.

Grisham bellowed orders to his people. Those tasked with moving the coffin to safety heaved it onto the waiting cart and pushed it to a corner of the altar, away from the chaos that was about to ensue. The front doors slammed shut as the guards on the stairs retreated inside ahead of the mob. That was an unexpected twist, and he felt a grim amusement at the elegance of the play. While he'd luxuriated in his confidence about the numbers, the Atlantean wenches had whipped up cannon fodder. When this was over, he would enjoy watching Ozahl torture every secret they held out of them for as long as the magical could keep them from expiring.

But first, he had to rally the rest of his gang. "Make a semicircle around the doors. Use the pews for cover." He took a position as far from the entrance as possible, shielded by the heavy marble altar on which the casket had rested. Several weapons were stashed at his feet, and he lifted an automatic rifle to his shoulder to sight down the center aisle. His people hunkered behind the wooden seats seconds before the doors broke under the weight of the bodies that pushed against them. They'd never been designed for serious defense and it was beyond their ability to resist a dozen angry citizens determined to overcome them.

He'd searched for options to avoid shooting his fellow humans since he'd first received the report of them gathering outside but had been unable to come up with anything. *And I definitely won't let them stop me from killing the damned Atlanteans.* He squeezed the trigger and stitched bursts of bullets across the three in the middle. At his action, his teams opened fire and the initial wave fell in no time. When they fired at the second, though, translucent barriers shimmered into existence to protect them.

With a curse, he ejected the magazine and snatched the one filled with anti-magic bullets that lay at the base of his cover. By the time he had it loaded, the newcomers were too close to his forces for him to shoot cleanly. He looked at his teams on the balcony who hadn't yet engaged and nodded at the closest one. She passed the word to her comrades before she aimed her rifle into the melee and fired into the rear ranks of the enemy and those who weren't already in close combat with Zatora defenders. The distraction allowed his troops on the floor to rally, and they fell back to the sides, which left him firing lines down the center to engage more of the Atlanteans' proxies.

In the next moment, the pews themselves became airborne and hurtled toward him and the people on the upper level, and he ducked behind cover. Apparently, they'd exhausted their supplies of pawns because the magicals had clearly entered the playing field.

Ozahl didn't react to the magic below as the folks inside the cathedral would already know about it. He sensed the distraction he'd told Danna to create begin to come to life and broke out of his trance in feigned panic. "There—

over there...something big is coming!" On the side of the building opposite the square, a fireball suddenly appeared. "Go, let's go!" He lurched to his feet and ran toward it.

His guards bolted to their feet and one pushed ahead while the other remained only a few steps in front of him to report the incident to whoever he was in contact with downstairs. When they approached the sniper position, he feigned a cramp in his leg and stopped. The man closest turned to look at him and reeled as a force bolt struck him in the face. He tumbled and Ozahl blasted the second guard in the back of the head and delivered a fireball into the sniper and his spotter on the corner.

He shouted in pretended alarm and scrambled up the middle incline as he yelled, "Someone down there killed them!" The other sniper team shifted their gaze to look for the danger and he incinerated them as well. He leapt off the back of the building, used force magic to control his descent, and landed cleanly on the ground below. When he turned, he located the two guards positioned at the outside of the rear entrance, who cringed close to the structure and looked for an enemy. He sprinted to them and shouted for them to open the door.

They complied and he kept the satisfied grin off his face. The first part of his plan—which had nothing in common with the ones the Zatoras or the Atlantean gang followed—was complete. Now, it was time to find his next target, one Jack Strang. The man had been notably absent from the site since Ozahl's arrival. His subconscious had chewed on that fact while he used his skills to supposedly guard against enemy magic and had actually been alert to the possibility that the Malniets would use this moment to turn the tables on Danna and her allies.

By the time he was jarred out of his trance, his mind had provided him with two certainties. First, neither Cali nor any other noble family was in the location—or, at least, they weren't using any magic nearby. And second, the cluster of bodies he'd initially categorized as part of the gang in the main room below were reinforcements for the Zatoras. He had to give the old man credit for hiding pieces of the plan from him. In return, he would wipe out those extra forces—starting with Strang, who was doubtless leading them.

Usha wrapped herself in a force shield as she marched toward the entrance to the cathedral. The initial push had forced the defenders back and allowed her people to gain a foothold in the space. An illusion sprang to life around her, the shimmer of which no one would notice in the chaos inside the doors. She was careful to avoid firing lines and to dodge the bodies that careened through the opening or fell onto the steps. Grisham was positioned at the far end of the hall but it would be impossible to reach him easily given the barrage of lead exchanged through the room.

She looked up and located the first enemy on the balcony to her left. He fired down with a rifle to target Atlanteans as they defeated their closest Zatora opponents. She raised a hand, reached out with her telekinesis, and used it to yank his weapon forward. The strap pulled him over the edge and he plummeted with a shrill scream. One of her gang blasted him with fire magic.

With space created for her by his demise, she triggered a force-assisted leap to reach the higher level. No one reacted to her landing and three enemies stood ahead of her, all with their attention focused on the battle below. She felt a surge of satisfaction as she drew her sword from its sheath, something she hadn't done except during training in years. Usha surged forward and channeled her speed and momentum to slice the first without warning, stab the second before he could do more than flinch at her approach, and sever an arm from the third as he twisted to bring his rifle to bear. She spun and delivered a back-hook kick to his head that launched him over the railing and into the melee below.

When she looked away from the fallen man, Grisham's gaze was on hers. He smiled in recognition and pulled the trigger on his weapon. It was the first time she'd ever seen a rocket launcher in real life and the way the missile grew in her vision as it approached was almost beautiful. She threw herself back with a scream and a call for her magic. The explosive detonated, exploded a hole in the wall, and collapsed half of the balcony to the floor below.

CHAPTER FIFTEEN

Rion Grisham bared his teeth in a fierce grin as he watched the balcony crumble. It was the first time since the tavern that he'd set his eyes on the witch, and watching her scramble and run was as pleasant as he could have imagined it would be.

Hopefully, I got her. I won't be stupid enough to go find out, though. The battle had devolved into individual fights, and his safety had to be his primary consideration. As long as he lived, the Zatora organization lived, so his death was doubtless one of the main points of this exercise.

I gotta hand it to the wench. Using the mob was a good play. He had another card left in his hand, however. He yanked the walkie-talkie from his belt and shouted, "Now," to the man on the other end. The affirmative reply was immediate. He shoved the device into his pocket and yanked the pistols from the weapons stash at his feet. *You can never have too many guns.* They were the same model as those in his shoulder holsters and filled with anti-magic rounds.

He set one on the surface in front of him as he

popped the magazine out of the other to verify that the bullets had their telltale blue mark, then repeated the process with the second. Part of him wanted to charge into the fray and get personal payback from the damned Atlanteans, but the rational portion of his brain prevailed.

There will be more than enough time for revenge later. He remained crouched behind the marble block and swiveled his head methodically from side to side while he waited for his ace in the hole to appear.

Danna fought her own battle on the opposite side of the room when the rocket struck the balcony. She knew with a certainty that Usha must have been the target, despite a complete lack of evidence to support it. *Other than the fact that Grisham would be dying to use his heavy artillery on one or both of us.* She detonated a force blast that careened her opponent and both enemies and allies nearby away from her and raced to the rubble along the far wall.

The sound of rounds smacking into the wooden pews behind her made her run faster and she cast a shield around her in case. If the bullets were anti-magic, it wouldn't help, but surely not every Zatora had the rare ammunition. It was a reasonable precaution, and only her fears for Usha had stopped her from thinking of it before she'd thrown herself out into the open.

The rubble was already shifting when she arrived. She used telekinesis to lift heavy pieces out of the way and in no time at all, had freed her friend. Surprisingly, a wide grin had appeared on Usha's face. With a shake of her head, she asked, "Are you insane?"

The other woman laughed. "Maybe. I'll let you know once this is over." They turned together in response to a loud explosion from the far side of the room and near the front. Where a door had stood, only flaming wreckage remained and a large group of people streamed through the opening. Her boss patted her on the shoulder. "That's your problem. Grisham's mine."

"If you think he's your only problem, we should talk. I've compiled a list. You have many, many more."

The woman straightened once she'd retrieved her sword. "It's a date. Right after we wipe these idiots out." She darted to the left to pursue her target.

Danna sighed in a mixture of amazement, disbelief, and the recognition that this was exactly what she should have expected from the other woman. "Fine. I guess I'll go give the newcomers a proper welcome."

Ozahl managed to fell the last couple of men from the reserve group with a lightning blast and they twitched bizarrely at his feet. He snarled in frustration at the timing of his arrival and his stupid reflex attack and moved forward cautiously in case his actions had been noticed. As soon as he stepped into the open, a bullet drove through his magical shield and caught him in the chest. He rolled out of the way of the barrage and called a wall of force to block the entrance to the passage his targets had emerged from.

The pain was intense despite the bulletproof vest. He guessed the shot had probably cracked a rib, at least, and focused on controlling his breathing while he took a healing potion from his pocket and drank only enough of it to fix whatever had been broken. Common sense reminded him that he couldn't afford to waste even a drop since he couldn't know what awaited him in the room beyond. One thing was certain, though. Now that he'd been seen attacking Zatoras, his time as a mole inside the organization had ended.

He pushed himself to his feet and muttered, "And good riddance." It took only a moment to change the face he wore so he wouldn't be easily recognized by those he'd betrayed before he picked up a rifle from one of the fallen men. No one would expect a mage to carry a weapon, which might give him an edge if anyone chose to engage him—or at least enough of one to eliminate them with magic before they realized he wasn't human.

After a deep breath, he released the magical barrier and waited several moments, but nothing happened. Finally, he risked a look around the corner and found the hall empty. He'd lost track of the bigger picture while he dealt with his issues, but as he walked forward, the sounds of battle, anger, and pain reached his ears. He'd hoped for a nice bottleneck, but the delay had allowed the reserve force to spill into the main room.

Fine. It'll be more fun facing all the Zatoras rather than only a handful. He launched a ball of force into the ear of the closest human, who fired his rifle toward the center of the room. His target collapsed with his skull broken.

A bald head appeared in his view and vanished equally

as suddenly, and Ozahl grinned. "There you are, Jack. I've been looking for you."

Danna launched herself over the battle to cross above the melee. Halfway to her destination, she locked gazes with a Zatora on the far balcony in the instant before he shot her. The pain when the anti-magic bullets struck her chest was bad, but the plates that reinforced the front part of her leather jacket prevented them from penetrating. The one that caught her arm, though, destroyed the material and buried itself deeply in her bicep. A wave of agony surged through her.

The distraction caused her to land badly, and she pounded into the far wall and lost her breath. She had the presence of mind to wash the enemies closest to her in flames before she fumbled for the healing potion she carried in one of the jacket pockets. Stars encroached on the edges of her vision, and she realized she couldn't draw enough air. The impact had obviously damaged one or both of her lungs. She swallowed the liquid and spilled some over her face in her haste to start it working.

A warm rush accompanied her body repairing itself. She snatched the energy potion from a different pocket, swallowed that too, and leapt to her feet as strength surged through her. As her focus settled, she pushed her magic into her senses to give her a hyper-detailed view of the surrounding battle. An adversary close by was in the wrong position, and she side-skipped at him, swung her leg, and drove her heel into his extended knee. It shattered with a sharp snap.

Danna didn't see him fall because she had already turned toward the next opportunity. A dozen feet away, a Zatora raised his rifle to shoot at a downed Atlantean. She stabbed her open hand forward and fire erupted from it and rocketed into his weapon. The heat ignited the gunpowder in the bullets and the weapon exploded to take him out of the fight and injure both enemies and allies around him.

She honestly didn't care, not when she was deep in her combat trance. Her motion became only opportunity and execution, chained one after the other in a long strand of precision violence. She eradicated three more but was jolted from her detachment by the arrival of her lover, who wore a different face than she'd expected. He lifted his gun in mock surrender and gestured for her to keep doing what she was doing. She turned to find her next target with a grin. With him fighting on their side, secretly or not, the Zatoras couldn't possibly last much longer.

And I'll finally get to introduce our mole to Usha when this is all over.

Ozahl stalked forward in search of Grisham's lone remaining lieutenant. He would have preferred to go after the boss but assumed that Usha would want to claim that particular prize for herself. *At least I can keep any additional support from joining that fight.* He battered every Zatora in his path with force bolts as he made his way toward the back of the sanctuary and remained close to the wall so those on the balcony wouldn't have a clear angle on him.

He found Strang in the middle of a triangle formed by downed Atlanteans. The man aimed a rifle at yet another one in the center of the space. A force blast spun the weapon out of his grasp and it clattered on the floor beyond. The Zatora lieutenant turned with eyes full of anger. It was downright rewarding to watch his thoughts play out on his face—the delayed recognition of the identity behind the changed appearance, the surprise, the disbelief, and then the confirmation of his suspicions. He mouthed something Ozahl couldn't make out and ran to the doors.

His blast of lightning went wide because someone bumped into him at the wrong moment. He growled annoyance and thrust the interloper aside with a burst of force magic, then raced after Strang and grinned. The headlong flight through the empty square headed toward Decatur looked awkward for the big-bodied man. A well-placed telekinetic yank on his foot brought him down in a tumble.

The mage walked slowly toward his foe as the Zatora lieutenant rose to his feet and brushed his trousers off. He seemed almost happy as he said, "So, I was right. It was you behind all this."

He shook his head. "Not all of it. But if you mean the death of Colin Todd, oh yeah, that was totally me. The hardest part was waiting for the right moment."

"Why? How did they get you to switch sides?"

"Since you're about to die, I guess you deserve to know. I was never on your side." He summoned his lightning, poured the power into the other man, and only stopped when there was no possibility of his survival. "I'm on my own side."

———

The battle seemed to be dying down but Usha didn't care. She hoped her group was winning but again, that wasn't relevant at the moment. Only one thing was—finding Rion Grisham and killing him. She had wrapped herself in a force shield to avoid unexpected attacks and held her sword one-handed and reversed so the blade pointed back on her right side. She kept her other hand free just in case.

A hail of bullets forced her into cover as the leader of the Zatoras darted up from behind his marble protection. She crawled toward the center of the room, hidden by the wooden pews that separated her position from his. Options for killing him were everywhere—the grand lamps that hung above the front part of the church could be yanked down and the large statues on their high pedestals could be toppled. If she wanted to, she could probably even hit the object he used for cover hard enough to crush him.

But, after all that she'd been through, she needed to make it personal. The fact that he was still around when he should have tried to run told her he felt the same. When she reached the center, she looked at the rubble against the far wall and reached out both her hand and her magic. One of the large pieces of stone, about half her height, glided toward her and hovered in the middle of the aisle. She stepped forward behind it and raced to the altar.

Bullets cracked against her makeshift shield. The impacts flowed through her magical connection and made her ache, but she maintained it. When she reached Grisham's cover, she leapt over it and released the stone to crash into the obstruction. She landed cleanly but he wasn't there. Usha dove forward as more rounds whipped past. Quickly, she scrambled to her feet and hurled a wide wave of force in that direction, and her opponent catapulted into the marble pulpit. His head met it first with a resounding thwack, and his face slackened as he slid down it. The pistols he held in each hand fell away.

The Atlantean gang leader crossed the space between them slowly, her gaze fixed on her adversary. When she arrived, he looked dazedly at her and a trickle of blood seeped from the corner of his mouth. He laughed hoarsely. "So. You outplayed me."

"You cared about the wrong thing. You were fighting for money and power. I was fighting for my people."

He coughed and took several moments to catch his breath before he replied. "Keep telling yourself that. It won't make it true."

With a sharp motion, Usha slashed the blade across his body to ensure he wouldn't speak again. She turned and faced the main chamber, where the battle had ended.

"Zatoras still alive, your organization is dead," she shouted. "Get out of my city in the next twelve hours or you will be, too."

CHAPTER SIXTEEN

"It's another fine day in New Atlantis," Scoppic enthused as he stepped into the kitchen on Monday morning. Emalia chuckled and Invel raised an eyebrow at the gnome.

"It is indeed," she said. "Coffee and tea are in the usual places and today, we have chocolate muffins."

He clapped enthusiastically and hurried to the low buffet that held the items. She shook her head and grinned at the elf across the table from her. "I had a feeling he'd thrive here. You too."

Invel nodded. "And this has clearly been good for you as well. It's not everyone who gets to have a private chat with an Empress."

She snorted softly. "Shenni's not all that impressive. Her time on the throne has been notable for political games but little else."

"That is the primary role of the monarch, isn't it? Making sure no one threatens their rule?"

"I always thought it was to serve the people."

He laughed. "You are an optimist."

Emalia nodded. "Guilty as charged. Speaking of which, we'll divide our tasks today. I need to spend time in the library looking at Atlantean history while you two continue to go through the things Cali found on Oriceran."

"What do you hope to find?"

She rose, refilled her coffee mug, and put her second muffin of the morning on a plate. "Options, my friend. I'm hoping to find options."

***

The mansion boasted several libraries, and it took her a while to locate the one she sought. It was more or less an official requirement that every noble house contain a set of the authoritative histories of Atlantis. They were produced by the palace each year and approved by representatives from the Nine. That meant there would be nothing particularly exciting in them, as anything controversial would likely be dropped from the permanent record in the process.

However, what she was looking for wasn't a matter of controversy, per se. One of the things the nobility embraced wholeheartedly was their connection to the traditions of Old Atlantis as well as those of New, and she hoped to turn that to Cali's advantage. A whisper at the edge of her memory told her something was there for the finding but unfortunately gave her no indication of where it might be hiding.

But if there was one thing that she possessed in abundance, it was patience. She pulled the first tome from the shelf and sat in the large wingback chair to read. The light from the window behind her illuminated the page perfectly. She wiggled to get comfortable and took a bracing sip of her coffee, which was positioned at her left hand on an end table. "All right, book. Tell me your secrets."

Emalia was yawning through the third installment when she found what she was looking for. It required rereading the passage a few times to be sure she had it right before she stood with a groan and walked as quickly as her tired body was able to into the kitchen. She assumed that if her niece was up and about, that was the most likely place where their paths would cross.

As luck would have it, both the girl and the Draksa were there, arguing over who should get the last muffin. The older woman shook her head and interrupted the disagreement. "I'll ask Invel to make another batch so knock it off, you two." She thumped the book on the table to emphasize the point.

Cali laughed, "Dang, woman, you're saucy this morning." Her red locks were a tangled mess and her shorts and t-shirt looked decidedly slept in.

"It's afternoon."

The girl frowned and peered at her watch. "Okay, whatever. Scoppic said you were reading history. Did you find anything interesting?"

She sat beside her. "I did. As you know, most of the established nobles love to talk about how awesome everything was in Old Atlantis whenever something happens here that they don't like." Cali nodded. "Well, it turns out that long, long ago, the rules of ritual combat were a little different. To avoid decimating entire families, the opponents could agree to end it with a single battle using selected Champions."

"So, kind of like trial by combat in *Game of Thrones*."

Her great-aunt frowned. "What are you talking about?"

Cali sighed. "Honestly, are you aware of anything that's happened in the last decade? Never mind. Keep going." She sipped her coffee and waited expectantly.

"Anyway. If the Malniets agree to it, you can end the fight against them with only one more battle."

She frowned. "Do you have any recommendations on how to do that?"

"A few." Emalia grinned. "I think I'll drop by one of the neutral houses and start setting the stage. You send a runner to request a meeting with Styrris this afternoon. My guess is that by tonight, the word will spread widely enough to reach his ears and he'll feel like he has no choice but to meet you."

The girl tilted her head and stared. "You're manipulative, you know that?"

The woman laughed. "It runs in the family."

Her great-aunt's timetable had been largely correct. Whatever she had done while she talked to the other houses resulted in an invitation to visit the Malniet mansion at nine that evening.

She'd considered what to wear for an hour and after coming to no particular conclusion, had gone through her mothers' outfits one by one. While it was an enjoyable way to spend time, she ultimately didn't want to play the game they expected. Finally, instead of putting on the trappings of the matriarch, she decided to go with a more martial approach.

Comfortable with her choice, she donned her combat uniform and made an extra effort to ensure that each of the compass patches was clean and vibrant. To the usual ensemble, she added thigh scabbards for her new daggers and positioned them on the outside of her leg beside the pouch on the front that held her potions. She wondered if her mother had worn the same weapons, perhaps hidden under the voluminous formal gowns the Nine had preferred at one time.

"Do you plan to talk to him or kill him?" Fyre asked. "The look doesn't exactly scream 'conversation.'"

"Either option works for me, but I've planned for the first one. If I wanted him dead tonight, I'd take one of the pistols and ask Diana for anti-magic bullets."

The Draksa snorted from where he sat near the mirror. His position ensured that she had to look at him every time she wanted to look at herself, which summed up the level of his need for attention quite well. "No one in their right mind would let you use a gun."

"Hey. Diana gave me one, remember?"

"Yeah, a stun gun. Which is all you should ever have."

She pointed a finger at him. "I'm sure it would work on you, you know."

He grinned. "Try it. You'd be an ice cube before it gets out of the holster."

"Go bother someone else, will ya?" She waved a hand at him.

Jenkins spoke in his disembodied voice behind her and she jumped. "Matriarch Caliste, your escort has arrived at the front door."

"I have an escort?" She frowned.

"Yes, Matriarch. It is customary. You would be within your rights to have one of your allies with you as well. However, having chosen to hold this meeting at his home, Patriarch Malniet is ethically obligated to see to your safety."

Cali and Fyre made almost identical scoffing sounds at the juxtaposition of "Malniet" and "ethical." "You know, that's a good idea. How about you ask Invel if he'd like to take a stroll? And Fyre will join me."

"Of course, Matriarch."

She checked her outfit in the mirror again. "I wish I had a sword. It would complete the outfit, don't you think?"

Her chaperone for the walk was a prissy looking teenage boy. His severe long black coat reached almost to his ankles, and his dark hair was slicked against his head. On a much older man, it might have been a good look. On him, it was pure pretension. She resisted telling him so but she and Fyre spent the entire trip commenting on it telepathically.

Mean spirited? Maybe. Necessary for our entertainment?

Absolutely. Besides, he's trying to imitate his patriarch, which makes him a chucklehead in my book. She also maintained a running conversation with Invel about his business interests and how she might help him expand them into New Atlantis. It was only partially show, as she was certainly willing to do so. But her other purpose was to ensure the opposing family's representative heard that she was making plans to be in the city for some time in case Styrris was under the illusion he could wait the situation out.

Upon arrival, Fyre and Invel were instructed to remain outside, as they were not explicitly part of the invitation. Both bristled, but she told them not to worry. "It'll be a quick meeting, I'm sure, and the family is on the hook for my safety." She looked at her escort. "Get it? On the hook? Because your family symbol is a hook? Oh, never mind." She followed him into the home and a servant closed the door behind them.

The entrance area was about the same size as her own —which essentially meant far bigger than it had any need to be—but much more lavishly furnished. A thick green carpet ran down a long hallway and about halfway down, an open door spilled a cascade of light into the otherwise darkened corridor. The boy stopped and gestured for her to go forward.

She considered the path ahead and whispered, "Know that if there's something bad down there, being young won't stop you from dying with anyone else who takes action against me." His eyes widened and she was hard-pressed not to laugh at the fear her completely false threat had engendered. *Like I'd kill a kid. Hell, I don't want to kill anyone.*

To appear unconcerned, she strolled forward slowly and peered at the art hung on the walls. The pieces were mostly hidden in shadows but appeared to be portraits with small metal nameplates beneath. The alphabet was again unfamiliar, so she assumed it was the Malniet house language. She turned the corner into the den and focused on the merrily burning fireplace. Two chairs were placed in front of it with a round table between them. She walked toward them and veered in the direction of the empty one.

The man in the other made no move to rise and merely stared at her as she came into view. He was light-skinned—almost deathly so—but dark in hair, clothes, mood, and voice. "What do you want, Matriarch?"

Cali shrugged. "The list is fairly long. I don't suppose you'd be willing to give me the information you know I'm seeking and let this be done?"

His smile was thin and condescending. "No, I don't believe I would."

She set her hand on the back of the empty chair and remained standing. "Then I guess I'm looking for vengeance, justice, that kind of thing."

He barked a small laugh. "So, will you attempt to kill me now? You won't leave the house alive. And those you love shall meet their ends soon after."

"Oh, you mean what do I want right this minute? Sorry, I misunderstood." She gave him a sweet smile. "Two things. First, I wanted to return this to you." She slid her hand into her pocket and removed the badge she'd taken from one of the troops at the museum after she and the agents had retrieved the sword shard hidden there. "I thought about giving it to the Empress as proof of your inability to follow the rules, but I realized that was probably what you were hoping for. It doesn't seem like you to make such a stupid mistake." She tossed it onto his lap.

He didn't rise to the bait. "And the other thing?"

"I've been doing research. I think a long, drawn-out affair that ends with me cutting through the last dregs of your family to reach you is unproductive for us both. I have other things to do, and you surely have to get on with…well, whatever the hell you spend your time doing. Matriarch Cormier, if the rumors are true." She shook her head. "Anyway, in Old Atlantis, ritual combat between houses could be ended by an agreement that a single battle would stand for all. I propose we do that now. My Champions against yours."

"How many?" His tone betrayed no interest, only irritation.

"Your choice."

He sighed. "I'll have to consider it. You'll have my answer within the week."

Cali nodded. "Sooner is probably better than later. There's no telling what might happen to your pool of potential fighters in the meantime. It could be they'll hear rumors of your proven lack of honor. Or about how members of your family keep dying inexplicably." She grinned. "There are so many possibilities, Styrris, and they increase by the moment." She raised her left hand from the chair, but the tiny listening device she'd pushed into the crevice at the top corner of the leather remained.

She backed away, her gaze fixed on him, then his silhouette, and finally, only his chair until she was out of the room. Once in the hallway, she spun on her heel and marched toward the open front door, where the boy who had brought her stood and watched her approach. A mental message to Fyre caused him to growl suddenly at the Malniet escort. When he turned in alarm, she slipped the recorder under the frame of the portrait of the severest-looking family member. She continued out the door and waved for Invel and Fyre to fall into step beside her.

The young escort moved as if he would follow, and she raised a hand without stopping. "If you leave Malniet property before I'm back in my house, your life is forfeit. Don't try me, cupcake."

As they walked on, Fyre sent her a mental message. *"You're not good at threats."*

She chuckled inwardly. *"True, but I didn't need to be good to scare him."*

"Petty."

"Yeah. I'll wear that."

CHAPTER SEVENTEEN

Usha portaled to the New Atlantis docks very early on Tuesday morning. She'd slept most of the previous day after the events at the funeral the night before, and her slumber was notably nightmare-free. Danna had led the charge to roust the remaining Zatoras from their hiding places and drive them out of town. The few who resisted, as she'd promised, no longer resided among the living.

Shadow loomed over the city, the dome's magical light source dialed down to provide the sense of a changing sun. In Old Atlantis, the rulers had experimented with extended days and even no nights, but the inevitable need for sleep had resulted in a cycle very similar to that on the surface. She'd chosen this time because she wanted to reacquaint herself with her home.

Although, strictly speaking, the domed city isn't really my home. Not yet.

Her family home lay in another part of the larger web of New Atlantis. Several wrecks had been connected by magic and technology to create a large space in which multiple families lived and worked. Many such collectives of varying degrees of sophistication were distributed across the ocean floor. She'd been lucky enough to be in one of the nicer ones.

After her departure to join the tournament to become Champion, she hadn't returned. Achieving the title meant leaving her past behind and she'd done it with her family's blessing, even though that required severing all ties. It was an old—and in her opinion outdated—rule. The Empress, however, had invoked it when she had pledged her service. As in all commitments to her monarch, she'd remained true to that promise.

Now that her people were on course to take New Orleans, though, she could see an end in sight. It surely wasn't too much to expect that Shenni would grant her some downtime in the small home near the dome wall, earned as part of the reward for her victory in the tournament. Even if she was to be sent to the surface again for a different task after the city finally fell under the control of New Atlantis, a break would be welcome.

Maybe Danna will come and stay for a while and we can explore this city together.

She hadn't felt this level of triumph since she'd been dispatched on the mission to secure New Orleans for her ruler. Meticulously, she had cleaned her combat gear before she donned it for this visit. It seemed only appropriate that she appear in her Champion's uniform to share the good news with the monarch. The sword she'd been given by the Empress after her pledge of loyalty rode in a sheath across her back, removed from its place of honor in her apartment for the first time in years. Still, it would be hours before Shenni would grant audiences, and she planned to spend the intervening hours soaking in the atmosphere of the city where she truly belonged.

Her chosen path followed an inward spiral toward the palace. She appreciated the irony as the street she selected for the last portion took her past the banners with the compass symbol of House Leblanc. The girl was still an issue but far less of one now after the elimination of the Zatora threat. In truth, she found much to like in the young matriarch. If destiny had not placed them on opposite sides, she thought they would have made formidable allies.

But some things aren't to be. She stopped at the inner ring to allow the guards there to question her, and they allowed her through after only a short delay. The "sun" above had mostly risen, and she held out a small hope that Gwyn might provide her with a meal—or at least coffee—while she awaited the Empress's pleasure. When she reached the doors, she found them closed before her. She nodded to the guard on her right, who was clad in shining mail that sparkled in the morning light and supported a trident in his left hand. "Champion Usha to see the Empress."

His deep voice expressed no emotion whatsoever. "The seneschal will be with you shortly, Champion."

I guess security has been tightened since my last visit. Maybe because of the rivalry between Leblanc and Malniet. She kept tabs on what went on in the undersea city, and that conflict was the primary subject of rumors and gossip at the moment. *That, and the whispers suggesting that the ancient patriarch of Malniet plans to wed the young matriarch of Cormier. It's like a soap opera here sometimes.*

The doors parted to reveal Gwyn between two of the Empress' elite guards. They were in the palace colors—deep blue and scarlet—and wore lighter mail than those outside and bristled with far more practical arms, including short spears, long swords, and daggers. The woman's face seemed to be filled with equal parts regret and conviction, but her tone was all the latter. "Champion. Please surrender all your weapons except the sword."

Usha frowned at the reception, which her status would normally have prevented. She didn't argue, though, and simply drew her daggers from their sheaths and handed them over, along with the belt that held her less direct threats. She scuffed a sole on the floor. "The boots have blades built in."

A flicker of unhappiness spread across the seneschal's face. "You'll have to leave them here." She turned to the guard on her right. "Get the Champion appropriate footwear. Now." He bustled away at her command, and Usha crouched to remove her boots. By the time she had finished, new ones had arrived in the same color and type of armor as the man wore. She nodded at the show of respect and donned them. When she was done, she straightened.

"Is this acceptable?"

Gwyn shook her head. "One more thing. Please turn."

For the first time in the process, Usha considered that something might be wrong enough to put her in imminent danger. Either of the men could kill her easily while her back was turned. Still, the desire to obey her Empress—

and by extension, her Empress' main underling—made her spin on her heel. Her sword's sheath jerked as they secured the hilt to its holder to prevent her from drawing it. While she could certainly free it, the delay would be sufficient for whatever guards would be present—and she was now positive that she would not meet Shenni one on one—could kill her before she could draw it.

Of course, I don't need weapons to kill. But they know that and doubtless are counting on me knowing they know that to keep me in check. More soap opera political nonsense.

"Please turn again," Gwyn requested and gave her a thin smile. "The Empress will see you immediately, Champion." The older woman turned and led the way down the long corridor and the brace of guards fell into place behind her as she followed. She'd already assumed they were headed to the throne room before they took the first corner that would lead them there. Extra guards stood at the ready everywhere, and she had begun to take that particular occurrence personally.

An unexpectedly large group crowded the formal chamber when they arrived. At least one male was dressed in house colors—*Cormier, imagine that*—and several others with no clear lineage had gathered around him. They might be merchants or nobles outside the main bloodlines, or who knew what else. She was positive that of them all, she had started lowest on the social ladder and was likely the only person who had truly earned her place in the room.

On the throne, her ruler gazed on her with a plastic smile. Usha had spent enough time with the other woman to know the real person behind the role she played. She was dressed in a long scarlet robe with a blue cloak covering a shoulder and an arm. Her tentacled hair was piled atop her head and seemed to writhe gently.

Shenni nodded at her and spoke. "Welcome to New Atlantis, Champion. What news do you have to report?"

She strode forward and gave an appropriate bow—shallower than anyone in the room would be permitted to offer save the seneschal and the main-bloodline representative from Cormier. "I bring word of great success, my Empress. The opposing faction in New Orleans has been crushed. Its leaders are dead by our hands. It is now only a matter of time before the city itself falls."

While she hadn't expected thanks, she had anticipated a kind word, congratulations, or a similar response. Instead, the Empress asked, "You do not yet have control of the city?"

Usha frowned as ice trickled down her spine. "No, Empress, but as I said, it is but a matter of time."

Her ruler's voice conveyed anger when she responded. "Well then, Champion, I suggest you get back to it. Do not feel compelled to visit us again until your work is complete."

The dismissal shocked her, but her body performed the appropriate actions, pledged to do as the Empress commanded, bowed, and backed away. Once she reached the hallway with the throne room doors shut behind her, the impact of her ruler's words hit her. She was essentially banished from the city and cut off from support.

Stunned, she turned toward the exit and her anger grew with each doorway she passed through—and many were present along her path. Gwyn intercepted her before she reached the entrance and motioned her into a side room. She complied solely out of respect for the older woman.

Once inside, with only the two of them present, the seneschal said, "My apologies, Champion. The Empress… has much on her mind at the moment. I am sure she will regret her choice of words in time." It was as close as the Empress' chief servant could get to criticizing her ruler, something Usha understood completely.

"I appreciate you saying so, Gwyn. However, I don't know that you're correct. It appears that things I once took as bedrock are actually sand."

"Times are changing, Usha. The Empress is caught between priorities. I do not claim to understand her choice in this matter but I am certain it is less about you than about the larger situation."

A sense of certainty about what she had to do came to her in a flash, and she stretched her hand to the buckles that secured her sword—the Empress's sword, really—to her back. She released them and pulled the sheath over her shoulder. To her credit, Gwyn never once looked fearful.

At least someone still has trust in me. She offered the weapon to the seneschal, who accepted it reluctantly. "This belongs to Shenni's house. It's time it was returned."

The woman nodded. "It has had quite a history, one particularly relevant to these times."

"You can store it in the palace where my Champion's weapons stand. I'll take them with me. Maybe put a little plaque beneath it. 'The sword that began the destruction of House Leblanc.'"

Her companion looked uncomfortable. "You know the girl is seeking the shards?"

"I do. And if she ever finds the truth, she'll target me—and your Empress."

The seneschal nodded. "What will you do now?"

"After we retrieve my weapons, I'll go to New Orleans and take care of my remaining business there. Once Leblanc is dealt with and we root out any hidden Zatoras, the city will belong to the Empress."

"And after that?"

Usha shrugged. "I'll return here and live quietly, I imagine."

Gwyn shook her head with a smile. "I can't see it, Champion."

She chuckled and the pressure in her chest diminished slightly. "Me neither, but it's worth a try, right?"

CHAPTER EIGHTEEN

Cali put her hands on the chests of the two wizards who tried to punch each other. Fortunately, they were both tall, thin, and more accustomed to magic intimidation than the physical kind.

"Would you two please stop?" She tasted only cinnamon on her tongue as her strange magical sense kicked in, which meant they were both simply messing around for the fun of it. Still, they had already spilled their drinks and risked those of several other patrons with their wild gesticulations.

"Knock it off," Zeb shouted from the front, "or I'll let her throw you both out."

She twisted to look at him and asked, "Oh, pretty please, may I?"

The wizards stopped thrashing, glared at each other, and turned to sit at their respective tables, accompanied by laughter from their friends. She rolled her eyes, picked up the spilled glasses, and returned to the bar. The dwarf grinned as she approached. "Don't you get enough fighting to resist feeling the need to threaten old men?"

Her snort made him grin. "First, those are two very accomplished wizards when they've had a little less to drink. Second, there's never enough fighting. Third, Fyre, bite the dwarf."

A soft snore came from the Draksa's position behind the bar, and she rolled her eyes. Zeb laughed. "He's on my side as long as my supply of soda water doesn't run out."

She sat on an empty chair while he made the next round of drinks for the customers in the common room. The tavern was less crowded than usual, and she attributed it to the uncertainty after the big blowup earlier in the week. She was very glad she hadn't been warned about it because she would have felt the need to intervene. That meant she'd probably have wound up either damaged, dead, or with a whole host of new people upset at her.

"So, has the council done anything but talk?" she asked,

He nodded as he poured the contents of an unlabeled green bottle into a glass. "Delia has secured her people's property and helped the gnomes do the same. I'm sure the others are putting their communities in order, too. Last I heard from Brukirot, he's champing at the bit for the name of someone he can target. Vizidus and I thought we should talk that over with you before we take action since the only real target is the Atlanteans now that the other gang is gone."

"Yeah, it would probably violate a rule to cut the heads off that particular Hydra at the moment." She sighed. "I'm fairly sure that even if I wasn't involved, I'd get blamed."

"That's what I thought. Oh, and Diana's partner Cara

was here with a man named Deacon. They did a security check of the tavern, your apartment, and the one next door, and the detective's as well."

"Great. I think they're coming to New Atlantis to make sure we're all good soon too. Why didn't they do Tanyith's place?"

Zeb laughed. "I'll let him explain that one to you." He finished filling the glasses on the tray. "Now go, do your thing."

Cali took the drinks and slid off the chair as she said much louder than necessary, "Fine. Keep your secrets. Jerk." His laughter followed her into the common room, where several patrons smiled at their antics.

The rest of the night passed in a pleasant blur. Cali's mind remained on her work and off the many things that tried to worry her. Zeb and Fyre held down the front of the house, and no one else tried to provoke a fight. Her only complaint was that she didn't have the chance to throw anyone out.

As closing time approached, Tanyith and Barton entered and took their usual seats at the side of the bar. She gave them a wave but kept at her job until the place was empty and everything was cleaned up.

As she slid onto the seat diagonal from the pair, Zeb pulled his chair over. He drew four glasses from his cask of homebrew and put one in front of each of them. She sipped it and found the drink equally delicious and strong. *I'll stick to sips, I think.* In New Atlantis, she was the legal age for alcohol and since she spent more of her time there than anywhere else lately, the dwarf apparently respected their traditions. The others drank more deeply, and the couple offered words of appreciation to their host.

Tanyith asked, "Aren't you past the point where you need the money from working here?"

Cali shrugged. "Not really. Even the recent bonus—" She stopped herself from mentioning the Zatora mansion, not knowing how knowledgeable Barton was. "Uh, isn't enough to make me feel secure. Besides, I have an apartment and friends here, and so on. Plus, I don't have as much time to help Sensei Ikehara, so I'll start to pay him for whatever days I miss." Her life was as up in the air as it had ever been, and although she could probably make it without the money from serving, it was an important touchstone to remember her true self.

She took another sip and changed the subject when she felt the weight of their eyes on her. "Anyway, what's this about not doing a security check on your apartment, Tay? Are you an idiot?"

Barton laughed, a deep-throated sound that conveyed a sense of satisfaction. "Well, there's no doubt about that. But I don't see what it has to do with his living arrangements."

"Ha, ha, ha, you're so very funny," he replied. "To answer the question, I…uh, moved."

The realization struck her in an instant. "Are you two shacking up?" They nodded. "Ew. Gross."

The others laughed and Fyre, who was faking sleep, sent amusement into her mind. Inside, she was happy for them, but she absolutely wouldn't let them know that. "So, what's the fallout from the big event?"

The detective frowned and sighed. "That was not a good night. The task force is still looking at all the evidence, trying to get a clear picture. The church folks are pressuring the bosses to release the building so they can start repairing it, and we're under pressure to go faster. All we can say for sure is what everyone knows. There was a big fight, magic was involved, and the Zatora leadership didn't survive it."

"And the organization itself?"

"It appears to also be gone. There is no sign of them on the streets. Again, word around town is that the Atlanteans gave them a deadline and once it was past, found whoever wasn't smart enough to leave and sent them to join their bosses."

Cali shuddered. "That's cold. I hope most of them left."

"I will say that the loss of life appears to be less than any of us would have expected. It looks like the magicals were mainly looking to eliminate the brains of the organization and fought only to incapacitate the rest."

"That's good, anyway." She drummed her fingers on the bar as she thought. "So, our friends at the Shark Nightclub have gotten rid of one set of enemies. That leaves them with the smaller gangs, the council, and me."

Tanyith added, "Us," and Zeb nodded in agreement.

"Okay, us." She shook her head. "I wonder how that'll play out. Maybe we should let the council take them on and deal with the fallout when it comes."

"You know you can't do that," the dwarf replied.

"Yeah. I do. But for once, it would be nice to throw all the pieces in the air and let them fall where they may." She took another sip of her drink and pushed it away. "Can you replace that with a soft cider?" He nodded and she swiveled to face Tanyith. "So, do you feel like going on a trip that will almost certainly result in danger and possibly death?"

He laughed. "Where do I sign up? You make it sound wonderful."

Barton frowned, and Cali thought she saw a hint of possessiveness in it. *Nah, I'm surely imagining that. Detective Kendra Barton has a heart? No chance.* "Where are you going?"

"China."

Tanyith coughed on his drink. "Come again?"

She nodded. "Yeah, that China. I started to tell you in New Atlantis but we were sidetracked. It turns out the scumbags who scattered the fragments of my parents' sword sent my mother a message telling her where one was—in the hands of a really scary person who lives in Shenyang, a city in southeastern China. I have to go there to get it."

"Is he likely to give it up easily?" Zeb asked. He set the glass in front of her and she took a deep drink.

"It doesn't sound like it. But Diana has agreed to provide both transport and help so we have that going for us."

"That's a lot and not a lot at the same time," Tanyith observed.

"It's a big task. But who knows? Maybe he'll simply decide to hand it over if we ask nicely." Disbelieving looks appeared on the other faces, and she added quickly, "Hey, it could happen."

Barton shook her head. "And when it doesn't?"

Cali sighed. "I can't save my brother without it. So, at that point, I'll do whatever I have to do."

The other woman faced her boyfriend. "And you're enough of an idiot that you'll do it with her, aren't you?" It wasn't a question.

"Guilty as charged," he countered. "And what kind of person would I be if I didn't?"

"A smarter one, that's for sure," she replied and swiveled to look at Cali again. "Try not to do anything overly stupid, would you, please?"

"When have you ever known me to be stupid?" They all tried to speak at once, including Fyre, and she raised a hand and yelled, "Shut it!" Everyone laughed, and she shook her head. "Honestly, aren't you supposed to support your friends? What is wrong with you people?"

She hid her grin behind the act of taking a drink of cider and sent a silent thank you to the universe for having such an amazing group of companions in her life.

CHAPTER NINETEEN

Cali and Tanyith had pulled together their battle gear and stored it in two large duffel bags, which they brought to the basement of the tavern to wait for Diana's team to open a portal. When the rift appeared, she looked through it and saw a strange corridor, somehow ancient-looking, made of unfamiliar material. Cara, Diana's second in command, smiled at them from the other side.

"Come on through," she called. "It's about time you saw our place."

They dragged their bags through the opening, Fyre crossed immediately after, and it closed behind them. The hallway they were in ended in a heavy door, and their guide led them toward it. Beyond was a small room with a bed, a dresser, and little else. Cara said, "Cali, this is yours. Drop your stuff here and we'll head to Tanyith's."

Impressed by their willingness to give her a space, however temporary, she obeyed. A right turn and a short walk took them to Tanyith's room, and he left his bag there as well. Cara led them out of the area through a door that led to a larger hallway. She turned to face them, and Cali was once again momentarily jealous of her muscles, her long black hair that fell so perfectly, and her classically attractive features. "So, welcome to our Vimana."

"The what now?" Tanyith asked.

Cara laughed as she began to walk down the corridor. "Vimana. It's like a Kemana, only less geographically limited."

Cali frowned. "So we should be worried about earthquakes?"

The agent smiled. "Not exactly. The Vimana can fly, apparently, but we don't have the amount of magic it would take to make it happen. For us, it's merely a base that's well hidden."

"Where are we?"

The woman grinned. "That would be telling." They came to a large doorway and walked through it into a room that was clearly a technical area. A wide array of equipment stood on plain white tables around the chamber, most of it unrecognizable. The few items she could identify were both expensive and impressive. "This is Glam's lab. She makes and breaks things of every kind here." A blonde woman who every man in the universe would describe as "cute" rolled into sight on a wheeled desk chair and waved at them. "Hey. Welcome to my lab. Touch nothing."

She laughed. "*Ready Player One*, right?"

Glam pointed at her. "You'll get along with Rath really well." She looked at Fyre and grinned. "Hey, I've heard about you. The troll thinks you're awesome. His words."

He smiled and nodded. Cara shook her head and

moved to a different door. "And through here is Deacon's workspace." They entered a room with server racks covering one wall and displays filling the one opposite. In the middle was a desk with several keyboards, mice, and other computer equipment that she assumed was probably as impressive as the equipment in Glam's lab had been. Behind them sat a frowning man with dark hair, and he paid them no notice as he pounded the keys on his keyboard and muttered curses.

"He's playing Fortnite," Cara whispered. "There's a kid in Brazil who's making his life miserable. Everyone else thinks it's hilarious. When he's not playing games, he's a computer wizard. Literally, he uses magic and computers together."

"I've heard of that," Tanyith replied, "but could never quite understand how it worked."

"We basically feel the same. All that matters is that it does."

She led them into another hallway and Cali asked, "Who will come to China?"

"I will. Hercules will since he's our pilot and we'll have support from Glam and Deacon. But the others are all out working on a different issue, even Rath, so they can't join us." She grinned as they came to an otherwise undistinguished door. "But you have to meet the most important member of our team." She opened it to reveal a long-legged off-white dog with a long nose, who leapt up from a sound sleep to bark and wag his tail furiously at them.

Cali cried, "Doggy," and fell to her knees to pet him.

Cara laughed. "This is Max, Rath's partner in crime. He's a Borzoi."

The dog licked her face and bit at her ears, and she collapsed to the floor to protect herself. He barked and danced around her, which made her laugh even harder. In her mind, Fyre observed, *"Rather undignified."*

She replied in kind. *"Shut up you, he's adorable. Take notes."*

After a few minutes during which the others gave the dog some attention and the canine and Draksa exchanged suspicious sniffs, they extracted themselves from him and headed out the door. Cali shook her head. "You have quite a setup here. It feels like family."

Their guide grinned. "It's exactly that. We've been through so much together. Most of us are closer than siblings, at least." She tapped a small earpiece and asked, "Hercules, are you about ready?" After a small pause, she nodded. "Okay, we're mostly set. You'll want to sleep on the flight and you'll get some medication to help you with that. But first, let's have something to eat."

The meal had been good—including several fish dishes for Fyre—and Cara had shown them the rest of the facility after. The agents had exercise rooms, a training room with customizable obstacle blocks of some kind, innumerable weights to lift, and all kinds of other resources scattered around the place. Still, it seemed like they used a very small section of a very large...well, whatever the Vimana was. Their tour guide hadn't offered much more information than that.

They retrieved their gear and hurried to the plane. It

was unexpectedly huge, and the cargo area held vehicles and even more equipment. She guided them into the fuselage and pointed them toward cabins after she handed each of them a pill. "If you have any problems, move forward. That's the direction of the green lights." She gestured toward a tiny LED that protruded from the wall. "Otherwise, I'll wake you when we're about sixty minutes out so you can get ready."

Tanyith looked a little bewildered at the suddenness of it all as he asked, "How close is the landing area to our destination?"

"About an hour's drive. The plane is our home base while we're there. Hercules will stay with it in case we discover the need for a fast exit."

"Thanks again for all this, Cara," Cali said.

The woman grinned. "We consider it an investment. We'll be sure to use you mercilessly any time something is going on in New Atlantis or New Orleans, count on it." The agent made a shooing motion at them and moved toward the front of the plane.

Cali turned to Tanyith. "Sleep well, I guess."

He chuckled. "Yeah. I have to say, this outdoes all the other crazy stuff you've dragged me into."

"Somehow, I think it'll only get weirder."

Fyre snorted. "Epic levels of weirdness."

"Look who's talking," she countered,

"Yeah, the smart one."

She sighed and stepped into her cabin. "Get in here or be shut out." He complied and she took her pill and stretched on the bed like a good non-agent before she buckled the straps across her chest and waist to keep her from becoming airborne if something unexpected happened. Inwardly, she laughed.

Oh, I think it's a guarantee that something unexpected will happen. Probably any number of somethings.

As promised, Cara woke them before they landed. Cali dressed in one of her mother's outfits, a black suit with a matching blouse. She put on the fashionable boots her mother had left too and pinned the compass symbol to her lapel. It took far too long to get her hair untangled, but she managed it and pulled it into a bun. She checked the look in the mirror and thought she carried off "professional business type" fairly well.

From his position on the bed, where he was stretched with all four paws in the air, Fyre disagreed. "No, you don't."

She turned and ordered reflexively, "Shut it, you." When she realized what had happened, she asked, "Wait, you read my mind?"

"Yes, I guess." He flopped onto his side and looked at her. "You were thinking loudly."

"What does that even mean?" She frowned.

"I don't know." Fyre gave her his Draksa shrug. "All I can say is that I could hear you—like you'd whispered it."

"Awesome." She rolled her eyes. "Less privacy is exactly what I need in my life."

He snorted frosty mist into the air. "I bet Nylotte will teach you how to better guard your mind. Of course, that might require a higher level of intelligence than you possess."

"Just for that, I'm glad you have to stay in the car." She stuck her tongue out and headed into the corridor. Tanyith was waiting, dressed in his own surprisingly fashionable suit. She frowned. "Did the little woman choose that for you?"

His expression scornful, he closed his eyes and shook his head. "First, I have very good taste in clothes. Second, if Kendra hears you call her that, she'll shoot you—or at least use a taser on you."

"She's welcome to try. Heck, when all this ritual combat nonsense is over, let's set up a cage match. No weapons, no magic, and only talent and strength."

"Yeah, I'll get right on that."

She laughed. "Your sincerity is overpowering. Dial it back, man." Cara appeared from behind him and waved for them to follow her. The agent was dressed almost identically to her, except that in place of boots, she wore low heels and completed the outfit with a dark-scarlet blouse instead of a black one.

With a wink, Cali strode forward and Tanyith followed, and Fyre padded out of the room to join them. The agent led them to a large SUV, black with tinted windows, and climbed into the driver's seat. Cali and Fyre chose the back, which left Tanyith to ride shotgun. The broad ramp that comprised the rear of the plane's lower level descended to reveal a grassy patch with a dirt track ahead.

The agent gunned the engine and the car rocketed forward, and Cali twisted to look at the plane. It was in the middle of a wide field, barely visible except for the open ramp. She remarked on it, and the other woman nodded. "It has a sophisticated camouflage system, mainly cameras and displays. When it works, it's great, but if one panel is damaged, you're suddenly not nearly as hidden."

"Do panels get damaged often?" Tanyith asked.

She laughed. "Our work isn't exactly boring, so yeah, it's fairly frequent." As they drove, they talked about random things, none of them important. When they reached the ten-minute mark according to the navigation system, Cara turned far more businesslike. She pointed at the glove compartment and said, "The comms are in there. Find the one that best matches your skin tone and ear size and put it in."

He complied and handed the box to Cali. She selected an earbud and slipped it in. Chatter was already active and after a few moments, she realized it was the pilot Hercules and Glam. She repeated what she heard in her mind, and Fyre gave her a couple of slow blinks to acknowledge that he received what she had sent.

Hercules' deep voice reported, "The drone is overhead and I don't see anything of concern. How about on your end?"

"Deacon is tapped into local systems," Glam replied, "but he doesn't have any blips either. I have satellite, but it's less useful than your drone so that's boring. I think everything's on the up and up."

Cara explained quickly. "We made an official request for this meeting through channels that Peng would respect —the head of a criminal organization in San Francisco who owed us a favor. The rules are simple. If anyone draws a weapon, everyone dies. Anyone who survives on either side is taken out by the gang for breaking his promise for peaceful negotiation. Otherwise, we're good to have a conversation."

Tanyith looked half-shocked and half-horrified. "You people don't play around at all, do you?"

The woman chuckled. "Well, this arrangement is kind of weird even for us but yeah, our games are generally at the high-stakes tables."

The resort that had been chosen for the meeting appeared in the distance, a venue mainly for wealthy tourists in the style of Taoist architecture with a multi-layered roof that jutted upward at the corners. Fyre clambered into the back at the sight of a checkpoint, and she felt the tingle of magic as he veiled himself. Their car was stopped about a half-mile from the building, and when Cara rolled the window down, they were informed that they'd have to walk the rest of the way.

In her ear, Glam quipped, "It's a good thing you all dressed up. There's nothing like a long walk in high heels, right, Croft?"

CHAPTER TWENTY

C ali was impressed by Cara's lack of complaint as they crossed the distance to the resort. The grounds were immaculate and she could almost picture the clientele in vacation wear—which for some reason, in her mind, always included the slouchy boating hats rich people sometimes wore on television. She maintained a running mental commentary for Fyre about what she saw. Tanyith chatted to the agent during their walk and occasionally, their earpieces would carry a snarky comment to them from Glam. No one else seemed worried.

She, on the other hand, was full of concern. The Draksa's calm, sarcastic presence in her mind was all that kept her from displaying it. The main building grew larger as they approached, and she questioned whether she should have involved the others at all.

I'm sure I could have found someone to portal me to somewhere nearby rather than risking their lives for my brother's.

"You're thinking loudly again," Frye replied. "And we chose to be here. Stop being a drama queen."

"You're a drama queen."

He gave a mental snort. *"Mature. Real mature."*

The walk ended at a dark wood bridge that stretched over a man-made waterway. It was blocked by two men in black suits and sunglasses, who greeted them with aggressive expressions. In a heavy accent, the one on the left demanded, "Weapons."

She opened her coat to show she wasn't carrying anything and endured an overly friendly pat-down from the second guard. The process was repeated on Tanyith and Cara before they were permitted to advance. On the opposite side of the short bridge, two almost identical guards awaited them and a Chinese woman in a beautiful red dress stood in front of them. She had dark hair that flowed in waves to her chest and a smile on her perfectly made-up face.

With a slight bow, she said, "Your bracelets, please." One of the men stepped forward holding a lacquered black box, which he opened to reveal an ivory inner layer of sumptuous fabric. Cali slid the items off her wrists and set them inside it gently. The fact that it felt so weird sparked the realization that she hadn't been without them since the moment Zeb had gifted them to her. The man stepped away with the box, and the woman bowed again. "We shall take very good care of them and they will be returned when you depart. Please, follow me."

She turned and led them through the automatic doors, which swished aside to permit access to the cool interior of the lobby. Sunlight poured in through the peaked glass roof and its tinted windows reduced the potential glare to comfortable levels. The large area was notably empty, save for a ring of chairs and low tables set in a horseshoe shape at the far end.

"Minimalism much?" she muttered.

Beside her, Tanyith gave a small laugh. "It's beautiful, though."

"What do you think a room costs here per night? Like, a thousand dollars?"

Cara, who had probably heard her through the comms since she was a few steps away to the left, replied, "Money wouldn't do it. This is only for those who are invited."

She frowned. "Who does the inviting?"

"The government, usually, or those with enough power to influence the government."

She recognized Peng Jian from his pictures as he walked into view from their right and stood behind the luxurious seating arrangement. Two more guards took position on each side of him. Their dark suits were a marked contrast to his white one, the only color in his outfit a pale-yellow shirt and a matching pocket-handkerchief in his jacket. His face was strong, handsome, and displayed his Chinese ancestry in every line. What was most notable about him, though, was the way his eyes bored into her as she approached like he was trying to look inside her—and maybe succeeded.

When they arrived, he gestured to the chairs. "Please, sit." They complied, and she stiffened involuntarily as her earpiece cut Glam off in mid-sentence.

The woman who'd escorted them said, "All communications in and out of the building have now been eliminated. We are secure, sir." She backpedaled out of earshot.

The man took his seat and regarded them without

speaking. Servers bustled in and placed small ornate trays on each side table with hot tea and what looked like cold juice. He gestured for them to try it, and she lifted the glass to her lips and sipped. It was plum wine, sweet and very welcome after the long walk. She returned it to the table as the others did the same.

Cara broke the silence. "Thank you for agreeing to meet us. We are in your debt."

He smiled, revealed perfect teeth, and leaned back in his chair with a small cup of tea in his hands. His accent was minimal as he replied, "Indeed you are. Perhaps, one day, an opportunity will arise for me to collect what is owed."

The agent returned his smile. "Perhaps so. I fear we will increase that debt before our conversation is finished, however."

Peng nodded. "By all means, then, please share what you've traveled so far to tell me."

Cali had echoed the discussion to Fyre and felt his wariness through their mental connection. *"I'm with you on that, buddy."* The man's self-assurance was entirely intimidating. She was glad they'd decided the agent should do all the talking.

"We have discovered that you hold an item of some value to us. We would like to acquire it."

He laughed and sipped his tea before he replied, "I have many, many items of value. Some I treasure more, some less. To which do you refer?"

"A statue of a tiger given to you when you became the leader of your organization."

He tilted his head to the side. "That is one of my most valued possessions. What is your offer?"

Cara shrugged. "Ten thousand dollars, US."

Cali's breath stuck in her chest and Tanyith stared at her and looked equally shocked. *Holy hell, that's a crap-ton of money.*

Peng shook his head. "While I would enjoy the negotiation, the truth is there is no amount of money I would take for that object. Look around you. Clearly, I have what I need and more."

The agent nodded and paused to sip her tea. When she set the cup down again, she asked, "So, if not money, what would convince you to part with it?"

"This can't be good," Fyre whispered in her mind.

"Right?" she replied.

The man straightened in his chair and locked gazes with Cara. "There is another object I would accept in trade for it. However, that item also cannot be procured with money, else I would have it already. Should you acquire it, I would be willing to make an even exchange."

The woman mirrored his posture. "Surely a man of your status is able to get anything he chooses. What could we possibly do that you cannot?"

He waved a hand. "Let's say I'd prefer to use a third party for this particular endeavor. And since you have a need I can fulfill, perhaps you are the logical option to address my desire."

"We would have to know more, of course, before we commit to anything."

He stood and signaled that the conversation was at an end. "You may ask Daiyu for whatever you require. She will speak for me on this matter. Do not make the mistake of thinking there is the possibility of negotiation here. And as time passes, I may find another who is willing to undertake this task, so I would caution you against delay." He turned and strode from the room, his guards behind him.

The woman who had escorted them approached and said, "Let us discuss this in a more private setting." They rose and followed her across the expansive area and through a door whose material was so identical to the wall and whose fit was so tight that it was almost invisible. Beyond it was a small lounge with the same comfortable chairs, dim lighting, and a bar along one wall. She sat and gestured for them to do the same.

Once they were settled, Cara asked, "So, what is this task your boss needs taken care of?"

Daiyu smiled. "A rival organization holds an object that should belong to us. We can't get it directly for fear of an open war that would serve no one. However, if you can procure it, we all win."

"Except for your enemies," Cali replied.

The woman nodded. "Just so."

"What is it?" Tanyith asked.

Their host shook her head. "You will be told only what you need to know and only when you need to know it. Once you commit to the task, we will provide you with all we know about the location and the likely opposition. Only when you are inside their compound will you learn what the object is."

She scowled. "Trust issues, much?"

Cara raised a hand to silence her and spoke before the other woman could reply. "We accept the task. We'll need to return to our transport to prepare." She raised her palms and said, "I'll reach into my jacket for something. You have no reason to be alarmed." Her hand slid inside and withdrew with a small fabric pouch tied with a drawstring. "This is one of our communication devices. You or a person of your choice can use it to speak directly to me."

Daiyu took it from her and flowed smoothly to her feet. "Then you should go now. You will almost certainly want to act under cover of darkness and as Master Peng said, time is of the essence."

Their exit from the resort had been the reverse of their entrance. When they reached the truck and after the obligatory pats for Fyre from everyone, Cara flipped the armrest open to reveal a storage compartment and ordered, "Comms in here." When they'd complied, she closed it and sighed. "That will block all signals for a while. The car will let Hercules know what we're up to through a direct encrypted channel. From here, we'll assume the comms are vulnerable to others listening in."

"Then why did you give her one?" Tanyith asked,

The agent smiled. "Two reasons. First, we do need to communicate with them and after this is over, we'll change the protocols and render that one useless. We do it often. But more importantly, it's always active, whether they want it to be or not. The chances are good they'll lock it in their own protected box but if they don't, we'll be able to listen in to everything they say."

They discussed generalities on the way back, and when they pulled into the plane, Cara led them forward to a room they hadn't yet seen. It had displays on all four walls and a large table in the middle that was also a display. The agent spoke into the air. "Boss, are you there?"

Diana's voice replied almost instantly. "Go, Croft."

While she explained the situation, Cali sent to Fyre, *"We totally need codenames. You're Draggylizard."*

He sent a mental snort in response and bumped her leg. *"And you're Agent Orphan Annie."*

She tossed her head. *"You're jealous. You wish you had such nice hair. Or any at all."*

"Nope," he replied. *"I like having brains instead. But you know, if the tradeoff works for you, who am I to judge?"*

She tried to think of a snappy comeback when Cara's words shattered her concentration. "Yeah, it's what we feared. I'm fairly sure they're sending us after a Rhazdon Artifact. The woman is clearly a magical."

CHAPTER TWENTY-ONE

It was difficult to believe how fast it had all happened. Cara and Diana's team launched into action and in no time at all, a drone flew overhead, blueprints of the building were in their hands, and a heat-mapped count of the people within was available. They'd discussed bringing extra firepower, but the agents were dedicated to other tasks and with only twenty enemies inside, most of whom would hopefully be asleep when they gained access, it didn't seem necessary.

Cara had reviewed the plan with them several times. They would enter as quietly as possible and use magic and stun weapons to deal with anyone they encountered. If it all went sideways, they'd be able to go loud, but the best result would be in and out with no battles. She'd led them to the lockers and rummaged through them to find equipment that would fit each of them, so both she and Tanyith now looked exactly like any of the agents would.

Each carried a stun pistol on their hip, a regular one in a holster at their lower back, and a stun rifle strapped across their bodies. After a few minutes of practice, they felt they could draw the weapons easily. Cali's bracelets were hidden under the uniform fabric, and they each had potions available. The agent's pockets bulged, presumably with additional gear.

As night fell, they were on the move again. The plan was to take the SUV as close as they could before detection became a risk. Glam and Deacon had plotted the electronic emanations from the house and discovered their security cameras and sensors ran to a distance of about a half-mile, so they would park three-quarters of a mile away and head in. Cara wore the stylish glasses all the agents had, which allowed her to drive without headlights. They'd put the comms on as soon as they entered the car, and one of Peng's people had provided them with information as they drove.

Cali sent a mental message to Fyre. *"The bastards still won't tell us what we're looking for."*

"Control freaks," he replied.

She chuckled, glad to have the Draksa along. Cara had suggested he was too identifiable and should be left behind, but both of them had objected strongly. His proven ability to veil himself had sealed the deal. They'd wear full-face masks for the break-in to obscure hair and facial features and gloves to hide their skin color. The single thing they didn't want, above all, was to have the infiltration traced back to them. As Diana had said, "We all have enough enemies. There is no need to add one more. Let them assume Peng's people did it."

"Well, it's kind of true," Tanyith had remarked. "For the moment, we are Peng's people."

"Nope," Cara had countered. "We're our own. We merely happen to share an interest with him right now. As soon as that's over, no one will have an instant's remorse at winding up on opposite teams. For all his smooth illusion of culture, Peng's a violent warlord who deserves a bullet as much as every one of them."

The agent's strong feelings had stuck with Cali. Diana and her people seemed nice but they had a hardness about them that went far beyond anything she'd ever felt. *I wonder if that's how they were before the job or if facing evil all the time made them that way. And if so, what does that mean for the rest of us?*

Fyre answered her thoughts. *"Zeb had any number of adventures and he turned out okay, right? So, maybe it's a little of both, but it's not for sure that you'll end up the same."*

She smiled and patted him gratefully but didn't put her thanks into words.

The car slowed and stopped, and the other woman announced, "We're here. When you mentioned Peng, we did some digging and discovered he's been gathering artifacts. Diana's boss assumed the guy would make a play like this, which is why we were prepared for it. When we get inside, keep your eyes open. It seems easy but it might not be. At all costs, don't let them find out who you are, even if you have to kill them to stop it. You can't afford that heat." She popped the armrest and put her comm in again before anyone could reply. "On the move."

They covered the quarter-mile to the outer perimeter at a fast walk. Cara chatted with Glam and Deacon at the base and quickly found and compromised the security cameras with small electronic devices she shot at them from an air pistol of some kind. As Cali understood it, they allowed the techs direct access to the equipment through a relay in the drone above and at that point they could do anything they wanted with them. They avoided the sensors buried underground by snaking through a winding path. She sent to Fyre, *"I have to get a pair of those glasses."*

The veiled Draksa flew overhead and circled the installation lazily. *"I bet whatever they're doing with technology, you could do with magic,"* he replied.

"I'm not so sure about that, buddy. But thanks for the vote of confidence."

Finally, they reached the physical barrier, a high wall with razor wire above it. "Well, that's not real welcoming," Cara commented. "We'll use magic to go up and over. No wards are present that I can detect."

"Try not to smash into anything, Cali," Tanyith quipped.

"Shut it, you." In truth, she couldn't promise a controlled flight. *It's one more thing to put on the to-do list.* The others went over first and she followed on a burst of force power and landed cleanly on the other side. Exterior lights illuminated the grassy space in front of the building, which was a single-level home that stretched in both directions from a central entrance, and a long area also extended to the rear from the middle.

They'd decided to enter on the far right-hand side through a window and into a room that hadn't registered a heat signature all day. The windows were all shaded, which prevented the drone from getting a good look inside, but it was the only location that seemed free of people. Tanyith cast a veil over them all and they raced into position. When they arrived, Fyre touched down beside Cali.

Cara withdrew a small suction cup assembly from a pouch on her thigh and used it to cut a tiny hole in the glass. She handed the equipment to Tanyith, pulled a thin cable out of her sleeve, and threaded it through the opening she'd made.

"Okay, the camera shows it's only a storage room. I see shelves everywhere with what looks like boxes of food, plus maybe fuel for a generator or something." She retracted the cable and took the glass cutter from her teammate. A soft snick sounded from the pane—probably the result of telekinesis—and she slid the blade of one of the pair of daggers she carried between the window and its sill to lever it open. "Shut up, no one asked you, Demon," she muttered and returned the knife to its sheath.

Diana had mentioned that she and Cara both had weapons that could talk to them, so Cali presumed that's what the comment was about. It was preferable to thinking the woman had lost her mind, anyway. The agent scrambled through the aperture and the others followed. She drew a very dim lightstick from her belt and waved it to reveal the shelves she'd described.

"Okay. Cali, open the door," she whispered. "I'll go first, Fyre next, then Tanyith, and you. If we see a single enemy, I'll disable them with the stun rifle. If we see two, everyone fires. If there are three or more, it's time for an ice blast." She pointed at the door.

Cali crossed to it and yanked it open. The agent stepped through it and the soft snap as her weapon discharged was followed by the equally muted thump of something heavy landing. When the others had passed, Cali followed and saw the woman drag a body back toward her, its hands and feet bound with zip ties. She deposited it in the room where they'd entered and closed the door when she emerged again.

"Okay, there's no way to tell what's in any of these rooms so we'll clear them one by one. The drone shows only three with more than one person in it, so we'll follow the same rules going forward. If we're lucky, they'll all be disabled before they know what hit them." They proceeded methodically through the building and the spy craft above provided them with a warning of every presence in the house. When they'd completed their sweep, two things were obvious. First, the security was inexcusably lax, and second, they had come across exactly zero magical objects.

They gathered in the central area and Cara frowned with her hands on her hips. "Okay, what the hell, people?"

"Have you checked everywhere?" Glam asked over the comms.

"Am I an idiot? Of course I have. Unless it's extremely well disguised and doesn't give off any magic at all, it's not here. Peng's guy said it's jewelry of some kind but we didn't find it in any of the logical places."

"Do me a favor." Deacon sounded perplexed. "Go to the back of the central corridor and put your hand on the wall." The agent shrugged and walked in that direction and the others followed. When they were in place, he asked, "Is that the rear wall?"

"Yes. It's made of the same wood planks as the rest."

"There's a three-foot gap between your heat signature and the visible end of the house."

She muttered a curse and ran her hands over the wall. "I

don't detect any illusion, so it has to be something physical. Look around."

Tanyith found the trigger hidden behind a statue on a low desk. He pressed the button and a rectangular section slid aside. Cali stuck her head in and saw a dark staircase leading down. She moved out of the way so Cara could look, and the woman swore again. "Okay, we have a basement of some kind. Are there more heat signatures?"

"None," Glam answered, "but the drone's sensors might not be able to reach that far down."

"Yeah, I know." She turned to face Cali. "We have to assume worst-case—that we've been detected and reinforcements are inbound. This is obviously more than merely a house so we'll do a single sweep through the basement, fast and hard. Anyone we see goes down, however they need to. Choose stuns first if you can."

She led the way down the stairs cautiously but quickly. "Light," she ordered, and Tanyith created a globe of flame and threw it forward. It revealed a large room with mystic runes etched on the floor. "No one move," the agent said and they all froze in place. "Do you see this?"

"Yeah," Glam confirmed. "The computer is searching for matches now. It looks like something elvish but not in a language we have on file."

Cara growled annoyance. "Awesome. Is that thing in the middle what I think it is?" Cali hadn't noticed anything in the center of the room, so she stared harder until she finally saw it. A necklace rested at the center point of the markings, seemingly made of teeth. Some were human-sized and others were definitely not human.

Diana joined the conversation. "It has to be, Croft. Does it feel right?"

"Yeah, it does." As the other woman spoke, Cali realized her skin was crawling and presumed that's what they were referring to. "So, my thought is telekinesis."

The lead agent replied, "Agreed. Do it."

Cara sighed and said, "Okay, y'all, get back up the stairs and be ready to run." They complied and a moment later, she barreled toward them. "Got it. I'm sure we set alarms off now if we didn't before. Let's go—out the front. Hercules, bring the car to us."

They burst out the door and sprinted to the gate in the wall. The agent battered it with force blasts when they were still a fair distance away and Cali and Tanyith followed suit. Fyre flew overhead and added a barrage of ice to the metal. It yielded seconds before the car arrived, driven remotely by the pilot.

"Get in." Cara ran around the back, lifted the rear hatch, and slammed it shut again a moment later. She fell into the driver's seat and they accelerated toward the plane. "Hey, Peng's guy," she said into the comm, "Meet us at the rendezvous in twenty-five minutes." She threw her comm into the protected box and waited as they did the same. "We have an analysis device in the back. It's scanning what we took so at least we'll know everything there is to know about it before we hand it over."

Cali shook her head. "I'll never be able to repay you for this."

Tanyith laughed. "Think of it this way. If they'd managed to buy it for ten thousand dollars, you really wouldn't have been able to pay them back. Maybe they'll let you be the base bartender for the next century or so."

She let herself collapse in the back seat and rested her head on Fyre's surprisingly soft scales. "Cara, please stun Tanyith. He talks too much." Laughter was the only response as she closed her eyes and let the Draksa's breathing soothe her jangled nerves. She focused on the fact that as soon as they made the trade, she'd be one step closer to freeing her brother.

CHAPTER TWENTY-TWO

Danna and Ozahl had arrived for dinner together and the mage wore a new disguise that she'd never seen. This was the one they planned to show Usha and the one he'd use in most circumstances until their future was secured. He'd said he might go back to looking like Aiden Walsh after that but honestly, she was a fan of the current choice.

His body was the closest he'd worn to his real one in public for some time, as far as she knew. It was trim and athletic, more a swimmer's figure than anything particularly muscular but attractive nonetheless. The face, though, was very different. He had chosen a distinguished look, a little older than his actual age—or at least what she thought was his actual age—with a few smile lines at the corners of his eyes. His nose was sharp and suited his other features well, and the rings around his irises were bright blue. His sandy blonde hair was cut into a longish professional style.

He'd done away with the slouchy clothes his previous persona had worn. Tonight, he sported a fine-looking dark-blue shirt and pale-yellow tie, having opted to go without a jacket for the evening. She had chosen a dress, simply to provide a contrast, and the black sheath was snug in all the right places while it covered everything adequately. She wore dark stockings and low heels. Her healing potion was in her patent leather clutch, along with a lipstick and emergency makeup.

She had been busy with her responsibilities since the battle at the cathedral and sensed that her partner was bored now that his main occupation was no more. That had led to the decision to spend an evening out together like they were two ordinary people, more or less. She'd called ahead and reserved a secluded table at a local restaurant that served amazing Ghanaian food, heavy on the creams and the spices. The international cuisine options in New Orleans were something she'd miss when they lived in New Atlantis.

Although, as nobles, I suppose we can portal to wherever we want and whenever we want, within reason. They'd be targets once their work was complete but that wouldn't be anything particularly unfamiliar for either of them.

Over a basket of sweet sugar rolls and glasses of wine, they traded small talk, flirty lines of little or no consequence. She could tell that he itched to move beyond it, even though he did his best to hide it. With a smirk, she said, "Okay, you've done enough to earn your excellent boyfriend star for the day. What is it you're trying not to say?"

The mage looked shocked for a second, then burst into laughter. His grin showed his almost perfect teeth, although he'd given himself a single slightly crooked one, doubtless for the sake of believability.

His voice hadn't changed and was still low and delicious. "Well, now that we've crossed one problem off the list, it's probably time we took a look at the others."

She nodded. "You're right. It's been a whole five days since the big event. We're slacking." Her teasing sarcasm made him laugh again.

"You haven't been. But me, on the other hand? All I've done is try on new outfits."

"Fair enough." She grinned and took a sip of her Malbec. "So, what did you have in mind?"

"It appears our initial plan to destroy Cormier while everyone is distracted by Leblanc and Malniet is doomed. The rumors are that there will soon be a marriage between Malniet and Cormier, which doubtless means that if the ruling line was to falter, there's almost certainly a deal in place for Malniet relatives to take it over."

She frowned. "Do you think Empress Shenni would be okay with that?"

He shrugged. "Honestly, I imagine she's already involved and would probably try a double-cross. But that merely substitutes Rivette for Malniet taking control of the fallen house. No, we'll need to go in another direction, unfortunately."

They paused while their main dishes arrived—shredded chicken over rice in two different sauces. They'd trade plates halfway through so they could enjoy some of each. After sampling her food and almost swooning with delight, Danna asked, "So, that means Leblanc, right?"

Her companion pointed his fork at her. "Not necessarily. I think Styrris Malniet has made a grave error here. His own house is now in jeopardy as well. Depending on how much damage the girl does to him, it may turn out that his family is the one lost to history."

She considered his words. "How do we take advantage of that?"

Ozahl shrugged. "We watch and wait and see where we can strike a decisive blow to make things go our way."

"It might not be an issue, soon."

"What's up with that, anyway?"

Danna had told him about the intention to end the ritual combat with Leblanc but hadn't had additional details to share until the day before when Usha called her in to discuss their plans. It had been a pleasant couple of hours spent in the land of "what if," but they'd failed to come up with anything more solid than the initial idea. "We'll challenge her to a final battle and field our best fighters against her. Either we'll win—in which case, the fight to replace House Leblanc begins—or we'll lose, which means our group can't mess with the girl anymore."

"That doesn't stop you, though, right?"

"I left the rules behind long ago, love, as did you." She grinned.

His expression matched hers. "Very true. Okay, do you want to do a little rule-breaking before the fight? We could perhaps eliminate some of her supporters?"

She chewed thoughtfully and took a sip of her wine before she answered. "I don't think so. She's done well so far and I think maybe we should let her make an honest attempt unless you believe we need her to lose in order to reach our objectives. Now, quit hogging and give me your plate."

With a laugh, he traded with her. "No, not 'need.' It might be easier since there are so few left in the main bloodline and no ancillary ones, but we can always keep that as a backup plan. As long as we take action in the shadows, there's no reason to believe that Styrris and his clan are any particular danger to us."

"How about the Empress? If she's backing him?"

"She is an opportunist at her core. She'll wait until she sees where the current is headed and then find a way to steer it to her benefit. I can't imagine she'd risk herself to save him, even if they're currently working together."

"That makes sense. So maybe the better question is, how can we undermine Malniet?"

"I hear more rumors that suggest the girl has offered him a final battle according to an old tradition. It's a logical move since he has way more family than she does. There's no guarantee he'll agree, of course, but I do wonder if it would help him decide more easily to find some of those he might depend on in future fights suddenly unavailable."

Her grin immediately revealed her interest. "What do you suggest, exactly?"

He shrugged. "Some threats to get them out of town. Maybe light kidnapping if it becomes necessary but certainly nothing more than that."

"They'll be more likely to identify your disguises down there, you know."

The mage nodded and waited while the staff cleared their empty plates away. "I'll have to use a little stagecraft here and there, for sure, in case someone sees through the magic. It's not a problem."

"Okay, then. It sounds as if we have a plan."

"Thank goodness. I was likely to die of boredom if this period of peace continued much longer."

Danna laughed and they continued to talk about inconsequential things over dessert, exactly like normal people.

One day, hopefully, we'll be normal people who also happen to lead a noble house.

CHAPTER TWENTY-THREE

Emalia looked in the mirror and admired the work the tailor had accomplished. When she'd decided to enter the game on Caliste's behalf, it was obvious that some weapons would be required. While her great-niece fought with swords and magic, her battles would be with words and required the right outfits to enhance her credibility.

She'd done her research and found a designer on the cutting edge of Atlantean fashion. It had shifted from frilly to functional again, another turn of the wheel that moved between styles every five years or so and often brought back elements from the past or occasionally broke new ground.

The designer had chosen to blend old and new in this particular selection. It was a loose dress that fell mostly straight to the waist and widened in a flowing skirt. The pattern was subtle, turquoise on blue, and gave the illusion of sunlight filtering through waves. Metal compass symbols pinned a cape at her shoulders that swept back to hang to the backs of her knees. It was light and airy and would be at the mercy of any breeze. The suggestion had been made that she use magic to keep it in place, which was likely the point of the extra item—to show that magic was so easy for a noble, they could use it for their wardrobe.

It's showy but it's all part of the game.

To complete the outfit, she wore earrings and a necklace—both of coral and pearls—and carried a small purse on a golden chain over her shoulder. Inside were the usual things found in a noblewoman's bag, including a brush, makeup, a small vial of perfume, and so on. Hidden within the handle of the brush were two tiny listening devices and two slightly larger receivers. If the opportunity presented itself, she would leave them in useful locations, despite Cali's misgivings.

Jenkins spoke quietly from the corner of the room. "You should leave in the next few minutes to arrive on time, Miss Emalia."

She smiled at her reflection, which looked both elegant and confident. "Thank you. Please ask Invel to meet me in the entryway."

Calm and resolved, she walked carefully down the stairs. The heels she wore were a little higher than she preferred but essential to accentuate the cape and provide an extra illusion of height for the ensemble. The Dark Elf smiled at her as she descended. He was dressed in a shirt and slacks appropriate for the walk to the palace. As she stepped beside him, he offered her his arm and she took it and gave it a squeeze. "It's good to have you here."

He beamed, a look with more than a trace of roguishness in it. "It's lovely to spend so much time with you, my darling." He'd taken to using that pet name since coming to New Atlantis, and she found it mildly surprising that it didn't bother her at all to hear it. *Quite the opposite, really.* She wouldn't have thought she was in the right place in her life for romance but apparently, the universe had other plans.

"Charmer. Jenkins," she said to the air, "if I'm not back in a few hours, send Cali to inquire at the palace and at House Terriau."

The disembodied voice replied, "Yes, Miss Emalia."

Invel opened the door and ushered her through.

***

She left the Dark Elf in a small chamber at the side of the entryway. Gwyn had overseen the searching of her bag and his person and found nothing objectionable. The seneschal escorted her deeper into the palace and turned down a hallway to a part of the building Emalia had never been in before.

"Is this the path to the dungeon?" She quipped,

The other woman chuckled. "No, not at all. It's simply one of many meeting spaces. The Empress has decided to see visitors in this one today. She does change her prefer-ence from time to time."

Maybe because she wants to throw off potential assassins. I'd worry if I were her, the way things are going lately. "It certainly makes sense. She must get bored with the same routine, exactly as we all do."

"I suppose so, although she never complains of it. I, on the other hand, very much enjoy a change of pace."

Emalia nodded. "Which is also entirely understandable." They passed a washroom and she asked, "May I stop for a moment? My hair has an issue." It did, one that she and Invel had deliberately created on the way over. She pointed at the offending locks. "It will only take a second."

Gwyn smiled. "Of course." She took a position in the hallway that would enable her to watch as Emalia hurried into the small chamber and stood in front of the mirror.

She had practiced until she had the action perfect and now ejected the first set of devices from the brush handle and palmed them without discovery. Once she returned the item to her purse, she tucked the tiny objects into an almost invisible pocket on the exterior of the bag. She slung it over her shoulder, rubbed her palms together, and exited. "Thanks so much."

The seneschal shrugged and began to walk again. They made a couple of turns and stopped outside an open doorway. Inside the room, Shenni sat with the matriarch of House Cormier, drinking from small cups, with a teapot between them. The Empress smiled at her arrival. "Emalia, do join us. Gwyn, pull up another chair."

She took the offered seat, formed a triangle with the other women, and took the Empress's extended hand to kiss, even though the setting didn't require it. The leader of House Cormier was a mousy woman with brown hair and darting eyes, thin almost to the point of ill health. Shenni was dressed in monarch-casual, a long robe in the palace's particular shade of blue. Her ruler let the silence hang for a moment, doubtless for her amusement, before she spoke. "Brielle and I were discussing her impending nuptials."

Emalia smiled. "I had heard a rumor about that. Congratulations, Matriarch. I hope this is a love match as well as a political one." All relationships among the nobles were political and from what she could see, this arrangement was entirely that. While Styrris wasn't repulsive physically, the man's personality was unbearable.

The other woman returned the smile but it seemed forced. "Thank you. I know it's the right thing to do."

Shenni interrupted before she could comment on the wishy-washy answer. "So, what brings the representative of House Leblanc to the palace today?"

She shifted her position to face her more directly. "I have come with a request, Empress."

"Very well. Let's hear it."

"Butt out." She said it with a smile but it was, nonetheless, a bold thing to say to one's ruler.

The Empress laughed and broke into a grin. "Ah, that's why I love your family, Emalia. You have no interest in banter and simply go directly to the point. Would you care to elaborate?"

"Actually, I guess this involves the matriarch as well." She inclined her head toward Brielle. "House Leblanc currently has a disagreement with House Malniet. We feel the apparent involvement of the palace—which has been the subject of several rumors—would create an inappropriate imbalance and prevent Patriarch Styrris from making wise choices. Caliste asked me to request that you remain neutral in this matter."

Her two companions exchanged glances before the

Empress looked directly at her. The other woman's eyes seemed angry and pierced her own. She maintained a calm demeanor and waited for her reply. After a moment, Shenni provided it. "I'm afraid your matriarch's beliefs are incorrect. The palace has no role in or opinion on your endeavor. Our supposed 'involvement' is simply in the binding of the two houses, Malniet and Cormier."

She turned to speak to Brielle. As she did so, Emalia palmed the tiny listening device and attached it to the bottom of her chair in another much-practiced movement. She continued to lean forward to adjust the strap on her shoe, then straightened again. After a few minutes, the Empress addressed her again. "Was there anything else?" The frost in her tone made it clear that there shouldn't be.

"No, Empress, thank you." She rose and was escorted out by Gwyn. The woman seemed irritated, probably at her harsh words to her superior. When they reached the waiting room, she passed the second part of the listening device to Invel and blocked the transfer with her body, then turned to distract the seneschal. "You know, Empress Shenni should perhaps have a care about who she associates with."

The woman gave her a thin smile. "You overstep. I believe it is safe to say that henceforth, the only Leblanc House member who is welcome in the palace is the matriarch."

Emalia nodded. "A release gladly accepted. I will miss you, though, Gwyn."

The seneschal's expression didn't change. "Be well, Emalia."

Invel offered her his arm again and they exited

together. When they were out of earshot of the guards, he asked, "Did it go okay?"

She chuckled. "Oh, I'd say Shenni doesn't like me anymore."

He nodded. "What a horrible loss. My condolences."

"Indeed." She rested her head on his shoulder for a moment while they walked, then straightened again. "So, let's go make other friends."

In her research, she'd found records that clarified the betrayal House Leblanc had suffered at the hands of House Terriau. In simple terms, Elisinia and Thomas had trusted Matriarch Terriau to provide warning of any actions against them and that alert had never come. One of the later notes sparked her interest, however, as Cali's mother had written that the head of that house had sent word that she was not involved in the action and that others in her family had isolated her from the knowledge she would have willingly shared.

It was not unheard of for those lower in the hierarchy to play their own games. Sometimes, the leader of the house permitted it in order to keep their hands clean. At other times, they were truly unaware. Her goal today was to discover the truth from the matriarch of House Terriau. Along the way, she shook out the remaining listening devices and slipped them into the disguised pocket.

She arrived exactly when she said she would, and the door opened at her approach. Again, Invel was given a place to sit and relax and she was escorted into a different room by a teenage girl. Matriarch Icille Terriau sat in a wheeled chair with a blanket over her legs. Her burnt-orange dress reflected a style long past, as did the heavy jewelry she wore on her fingers and around her neck. Her white hair was pulled into a tight bun and her voice was as sharp as her mind was reputed to be. "Girl. Get us tea and cakes and be quick about it." She waved a hand at a chair next to her, and Emalia sat.

"Thank you for agreeing to see me."

The other woman snorted. "I have so few visitors these days, I would have accepted simply to break the monotony." She smiled and it seemed genuine. "But our houses have a long and troubled relationship, much to my regret. I would not refuse you or your niece."

"That relationship is what I'm here to discuss today."

"I thought it might be." She turned as the girl returned with a tray, which wobbled in her hold as she hurried to set it on the low table between the chairs. Sounding suddenly cross, Icille snapped, "Well, pour, girl. Honestly, where are your manners?" The young woman did as she was told and bolted from the room. The matriarch laughed. "She's been coddled far too much. I'll turn her into a force to be reckoned with, mark my words."

"Your granddaughter, I presume? In the main line?"

She nodded and lifted her cup in a trembling hand. "Yes. My daughter's girl. Her husband is an idiot—my daughter's, I mean. The girl's too young to marry. Anyone other than Styrris Malniet, anyway." She cackled gleefully.

Emalia couldn't resist a smile. "It is certainly so. And he is part of the reason I'm here, as well. May I explain?" The other woman nodded and gestured agreement. "The

Malniets have a secret we must compel them to reveal. At the same time, we also seek the pieces of the house sword that was broken during the…uh, incident." *I probably shouldn't use the word betrayal here.* "Some writings left behind suggested that you might have knowledge that could help us."

Sadness flowed onto the woman's face, starting in her eyes and ending with a frown. "I know what happened to the boy—the matriarch's brother. It's a terrible thing. And I hear your unspoken question. No, I was not involved in the action to remove their parents. I was not." She emphasized the last word as if arguing with an unseen opponent. "It was done without my knowledge. While I watched and waited, others kept information from me."

If she's acting, she's good enough to have made a career of it.

"Is there any information you can share now?"

The old woman shook her head. "My children might know. In fact, I'm sure they do. They're always in their room, whispering and plotting. I've tried to listen in magically but they're wise to that trick."

She grinned. "Would you tell us the location of the shard if you knew?"

"I would."

"Do you think you could inspire them to talk about it behind closed doors?"

The matriarch nodded. "Certainly. I could make them fear its discovery or some such thing but I don't know what good that would do."

Emalia slid her hand into the pocket of her purse, retrieved the listening device, and held it up for her to see. "I think I have a solution to three problems at once. This will provide a way for us to find out about the shard, a way for you to find out what they're talking about behind your back, and a way to help your granddaughter learn the important arts of secrecy and manipulation."

Matriarch Terriau's gleeful laughter was all the confirmation she needed that trusting her had been the right choice.

CHAPTER TWENTY-FOUR

Once Cali had finished a long tirade at Emalia about how dangerous it had been to plant surveillance devices in the palace and House Terriau—which the older woman seemed entirely unmoved by—they'd agreed to use the kitchen as the base station for listening to the information from the bugs. Since the arrival times were unpredictable and the knowledge they might gain was so important, one of them would always be on call and Jenkins had volunteered to alert that person if the lights on the receivers changed colors.

It was her turn for that particular responsibility and she was sound asleep when Jenkins' voice snapped her out of her haze in the middle of the night. "Matriarch Caliste, there's something on the boxes."

She sat with a yawn, dislodged Fyre from where he lay between her feet, and descended to the kitchen. Barely awake, she pressed the buttons to start the coffee brewing and settled in the chair in front of the black boxes. The

LEDs on the top of two of them glimmered green. She started the one connected to the bug she'd left in Styrris Malniet's den. The recording was of him berating a servant for bringing the wrong bottle of wine. She shook her head and sighed. "Well, that's useful."

"We already knew he was a jerk," Fyre replied. He had curled in his usual position beneath the table.

"We did indeed." She yawned again, rose to fill a mug, and looked at her watch. "One in the morning. Diana's people could have made this more convenient, you know?"

He snorted, and his frosty breath chilled her bare toes. "I'm sure your comfort is their primary consideration."

"Shut it, you." She grinned and shook her head to focus. "Okay, Matriarch Terriau, let's see what you have for us."

She activated the playback and a soft click emitted from the box—probably a door closing. Two voices, low and urgent, were clear and understandable.

"Why the hell is the old bat talking about the sword now?" a man's tone demanded.

"The aunt from Leblanc stopped by," a woman replied. "She must have put it in her head."

"Idiots. Both of them. But there's no way she could know where it is."

"My mother is many things, but stupid is not one of them. It's been hidden there for a long time. She might have worked it out."

He laughed. "She's in a wheelchair. She couldn't have gone out there."

Cali straightened in her chair, all traces of sleepiness gone, and pressed the button to pause the playback. "Jenkins, do we have a map that shows Terriau's property?"

"Of course, Matriarch. All the houses have maps of the city. You'll find it in the second-floor library in the bottom drawer of the cabinet."

She didn't quite run to get it but it was more than a walk. When she returned to the kitchen, she spread the large white paper with its black markings over the table. It took her a few minutes to orient herself, as the noble properties were only referenced by symbol and she hadn't yet memorized them all. Finally, she remembered thinking that Terriau should be full of knights and found the stylized helmet that represented them. Like her property, theirs contained several outbuildings, which might be what the two had referred to. She started the recording again.

"No, that's true," the woman said. "Still, if she's checked the ones on the path, that would tell her it could only be in the others."

"Only if she thought to look before," the man countered.

Matriarch Terriau's daughter laughed sharply. "Have you met my mother? She puts the busy in busybody and we've been too involved in other things to keep an eye on her."

He sighed. "I suppose you're right. There's only one thing for it. We'll have to move it."

Cali cringed, unsure of when the conversation had been recorded and fearful of what might come next.

But it must be from today after Emalia visited. Which means it should only be a few hours old, at most. They wouldn't have moved that fast, would they?

The woman growled annoyance. "To where?"

He responded in kind, "I have no idea. How the hell

should I know? She's your mother. Why don't you have control of her?"

Their argument was interrupted by a knock on the door and the recorder clicked off shortly thereafter. She gave Fyre a gentle kick. "Do what you need to do to wake up, buddy. Tonight, we get to be thieves." The excitement surged through her and she raced up the stairs to dress.

She arrived at the Terriau estate at two-thirty in the morning, clad all in black. The compass symbols on her uniform were covered by their patches, and she'd pulled a watch cap on to hide her hair. The streets were deserted, which allowed her to reach the perimeter of their land without detection. That was the easy part.

Her careful approach had taken her almost all the way to the rear boundary and close to the ring that separated the Nine from the rest of the city. A six-foot stone wall topped with wicked-looking metal spikes protected the property from trespassers. In the darkness, it looked ominous and brought memories of sneaking into the cemetery in New Orleans.

Man, that feels like a lifetime ago. She ducked into the shadows and sent to Fyre, "*Okay, tell me how many buildings there are that aren't accessible to someone in a wheelchair.*"

The Draksa flew overhead, hidden behind his veil. "*I see three,*" he replied. "*A big one at the back and two smaller ones in front of it. They have a path between them but aren't connected to the one that joins the main house with the others.*"

"That's weird. Maybe they had a disagreement at some point and dug it up?" The buildings on her family's estate were all easily navigable. *"Which do you think I should try first?"*

A wave of mirth came across the channel. *"Whichever you choose, it'll be wrong. So does it matter?"*

She put a growl in her telepathic voice. *"No one likes a smart ass, scale-face."*

"That doesn't make me wrong."

Cali sighed. *No, it doesn't. So we'll do the closest one first.* She looked around to be sure she was alone and built a staircase of force blocks. Her skills had improved a great deal since the night she and Fyre had met, and she scaled the fence quickly and landed on the Terriau grounds. She'd checked for wards but like her property, they had only secured the buildings, not the lawns and gardens surrounding them.

The one at the back was two stories high and built of what appeared to be white marble in the pale light from the dimmed false sun overhead. Windows were positioned across the second level at regular intervals. The only opening at her height was a heavy door made of dark wooden planks and flanked by carvings of the family's symbol with both helmets facing inward. She moved into the shadows cast by a large tree that grew beside the structure and opened her senses.

Magic radiated from the building, which indicated at least one strong ward. *I wish Zeb or Nylotte were here. They're so much better at this than I am.*

"Everyone is," Fyre replied. *"You're terrible at wards. Oh, and you're thinking loudly again."*

She couldn't help but chuckle at the Draksa's unending snark. *"Shut it, you. I'm trying to work. You make sure you'll be ready to cause a distraction if I screw up."* The backup plan was for him to fly through the property and trip all the wards from as high as he could so he wouldn't be caught. She'd use the time to finish her search as quickly as possible.

But if I get it right, that won't be necessary. So, let's get it right.

Refocused, she switched from passive reception to active magic to poke and prod gently at the ward to get a sense of how it had been created. After a few minutes, she realized it exceeded her ability to untangle it. However, those who had placed it had done so with magical threats in mind, which meant the wards would only detect the use of magic. Several of those on her property had been the same before Zeb fixed them.

I guess we all have our blind spots. Maybe Atlantean culture is so tied to magic they can't imagine anything different. She chuckled. *Dasante would make a killing here with his three-card monte. They'd be searching for magic while he used sleight of hand to rob them blind.*

She circled to the back of the building in search of a way inside that didn't involve the use of magic. "Fyre, can you see through the windows?"

After a short delay, she felt the air move as he flew above her. "No, they're all tinted."

"Damn. Okay." She had run out of options, but the crazy idea that slid into her head inspired her to keep looking. After a couple of minutes, she realized she had no other choice.

"Hey, buddy. Do you think you can lift me?"

It took a fair amount of coordination and the process wasn't elegant, but the Draksa was able to carry her while she maintained a death grip on his front paws. He hauled her to the roof, and she barely managed to avoid sliding off the edge when she released her hold and the ceramic tiles broke under her feet. She hung by her fingers off the back of the building, facing a window. Once she'd caught her breath, she drew a dagger out of its sheath with one hand and shattered the glass. It fell inward with a shower of small sounds. She could make out shelves and other shapes, but the room was too dim to accurately identify anything.

It took a moment to clear the remainder of the slivers from the frame, and she eased herself in slowly, hung for a moment, and finally dropped the last several feet to the floor. She rolled and came up in a crouch, ready to deal with anything that might accost her in the darkness. Nothing did, and she waited in stillness for her eyes to adjust. When she could finally see, she confirmed that the area was a large storage room, although a heavy bag attached to a mount in the corner suggested that at one time, it could have been an exercise space.

That would explain the windows, anyway.

Heavy canvas tarps covered everything, and she pulled them off one after the other. Dust rose and settled with each movement. She revealed boxes, pieces of old furniture, and even a footlocker filled with clothes that looked a century out of date.

"Have you found anything?" Fyre asked.

She yanked the second to last tarp aside and revealed a tall wardrobe. It had a lock on it, the first she'd seen in the building. "Maybe." A chain was threaded through the handles of the doors and while she was no good at lock-picking, the screws that held the metal braces in place were a point of vulnerability. Quickly, she retrieved the multi-tool she'd taken from the go-bags her parents had left from her belt, folded the screwdriver open, and went to work. Minutes later, she had removed the handle and the door fell open.

Within lay a fabric-wrapped bundle, longer than it was wide. She held her breath, removed the covering, and sighed with relief. "I've got it." She folded the cloth around it and turned to the main entrance. "And I think I'd like to leave a message."

The wards had been designed to do two things. The first was to sound an alarm in the event of magic use. They did that job perfectly and a flood of people raced out of the mansion in their pajamas after what she considered an impractical delay. The second was that they were supposed to suppress the magic used so that the offender could be caught while they tried to determine why their power wasn't working.

They successfully absorbed her first burst of force magic, but when Fyre flew in and iced the door and she followed up with a bolt of lightning, the combination over-whelmed the defenses and cracked the wood. Her next force blast hurled it free, and she turned and lobbed a fire-ball into the building before she launched herself over the fence. Somehow, despite the destruction, she thought Matriarch Icille Terriau would be laughing.

CHAPTER TWENTY-FIVE

Usha's emotional state was volatile, to put it mildly. At some moments, she was almost giddily happy and flushed with the success of her victory over the Zatoras. At others, she veered to the opposite side of the spectrum and was overwhelmed by sadness over the Empress's behavior toward her. It was an uncomfortable combination, and the only way she could cope with it was by taking action.

After a few days of rest, she'd sent her people out to expand their territory. The minnows that had nibbled at the gang before were given three options—become a vassal of the organization, leave town immediately, or die. About an equal number selected the first two and sadly, some forced them to apply the third. The overall situation became more stable by the day.

The Zarcanum supply had been restored and despite feeling unwell in the recent past, most of the clientele were eager to start using again. She'd banished the spell that activated the magic in the drugs so no ill effects would occur. Shine continued to sell, but its purpose now was merely cash flow and dependency. She didn't envision a situation where she'd have to create a mob again. Still, it was good to know that she had the option if it was needed.

That left only the council and Leblanc. She imagined that Shenni would tell her to focus on the former because the Malniets might deal with the latter, based on everything she heard. But she had no interest in doing so. She wanted that fight and even craved it. And if victory didn't come, her options would be substantially narrowed. Either she'd be dead—which she neither preferred nor feared—or she'd be unable to target the girl any longer and would be free to turn her attention elsewhere.

Accordingly, she sat at the bar of the Shark Nightclub at nine in the morning on a Saturday, waiting for her second in command to arrive. A single worker was present, setting up for the day, and kept her supplied with a continuous flow of hot coffee. She imagined there was work she could do while she waited but none of it seemed to matter at the moment. The battle ahead was one she couldn't see past. Or, maybe, didn't want to see past.

Either way, I'll take it.

She'd found a purity of purpose again, if only for a short time, and liked the feeling. When the front door opened and spilled light into the room, she squinted against it and smiled at the silhouette framed in the aperture. The door closed to reveal the woman dressed uncharacteristically in jeans and a man's button-down shirt. It was suspicious and she grinned.

"That's not your shirt, is it? This is a walk of shame moment."

Danna shook her head as she sat on the stool beside her and accepted a steaming cup of coffee gratefully. She drank deeply, then grinned. "I will neither confirm nor deny. How about you. What makes you drag me in here this early and with only an hour's notice, no less?"

Usha laughed. "Maybe I simply wanted to see what you were like on a Saturday morning when you didn't have time to prepare." She shook her head. "No, it's that I've come to a decision and I need to talk to you about it."

The woman nodded. "Shoot."

"We'll end it with the girl. Now—well, a week from now. That's about the earliest we can legitimately make it."

"Okay. You know I'm in. What's the plan?"

"We'll need the best people we can find. Who's left?"

Her companion sighed. "After last Sunday, we're not at our best. I don't suppose you'd want to delay it?" She raised an eyebrow, and Danna laughed. "Yeah, I didn't think so. Okay. We are up to six by the rules and need a minimum of four to match what she brought last time. One of the Empress's enforcers is still here and he's worth including. Other than that, we have a shit-ton of average people who are dependable, plus Bear."

She grinned at the mention of the Shark's main bouncer, a burly man who spent his free time—all of it— lifting weights and participating in underground fights. He had powerful magic but most of the time, he was so excited to fight with his fists that he didn't think to use it. All that meant he was an absolute wildcard and perfect for the bout. "You can stop there," she said. "We'll do four on four. You, me, the enforcer, and Bear."

Her second straightened. "Now that's what I like to hear. It's about time you let me take a crack at her."

"I couldn't risk you before the final fight as I needed you too much. I still do, but we'll be together so whatever happens will happen to both of us. We'll decide where we go from there depending on the result."

"Excellent."

Usha smiled. "So, do you want to tell me more about last night?"

The woman laughed and shook her head. "Let's get the battle behind us. Then, all my secrets will be revealed."

"Fair enough."

Tanyith packed the last bag from his apartment and gave it one final check. He chuckled and said, "She's right. This place is a hole." He wouldn't miss it. In the back of his mind, he wondered if maybe he'd deliberately avoided putting roots down in the hopes that things would turn out this way with Kendra. It was fast, sure, but his feelings for her were seriously intense.

She was at work today, exactly like every day lately. The events of the previous weekend and the Atlantean organization's activities since then had everyone in the gang task force on deck twelve hours a day or more, weekends apparently included. On the one hand, it allowed him enough time for his responsibilities and to get moved in. But on the other, he had hoped cohabitating would result in more time together than they were getting.

Extra work can't last forever, right?

He opened a portal from his old living room into his new one and stepped across. Kendra's apartment was about two and a half times the size of his, half of a duplex in the Garden District that had once been a much fancier home. They had a main floor, a top floor, and shared a basement. She'd separated the second bedroom to use as part-office and part-exercise space and had offered him the closet in there for his belongings. It had made him laugh. They were living together, but not completely together. It was a reasonable decision and kept things slow, steady, and easily escapable.

Although he had no interest in escaping. He hung the items that needed to hang, piled the rest of his clothes on the top shelf, and used a convenient hook to store the new daggers Cali had given him. He was trying to find a way to carry them concealed but they were a little big to do so easily. A practice session had revealed that he could channel magic through them, which would be a huge bonus in the inevitable next battle.

Or when I deal with the meddling Malniets.

He had contacted Zeb and asked him for non-critical information about the council and encouraged him to spice it up with falsehoods. He could delay incinerating the nightclub. Since the man had said a week, he planned to wait all seven days. He could avoid the other requirement until Cali arranged the next challenge against the family.

Still, he wanted to seem like he was compelled and firmly on their hook, right up until the moment when he dealt with them both. He and Kendra had indulged in a couple of conversations on the matter and she was fairly sure there was a place for them in one of the magical jails nearby based on the evidence he'd be able to present. Extradition could be a complication but not if Malniet fell.

Tanyith considered whether he wanted to potter around the apartment and try to do useful things. When he realized that the potential to annoy Kendra was greater than the potential to accomplish anything significant, he decided to head out for a walk instead. As he turned to lock the front door, a chill ran from the top of his spine to the bottom. On the white surface was a black envelope with his name on it. He opened it and found another envelope inside addressed to Cali.

There go my plans for the day.

He checked the tavern first, but Zeb said she was in New Atlantis. The dwarf looked more stressed than Tanyith had ever seen him, but from the way his gaze tracked Janice's movements, it was probably fear for his glassware. He retrieved the information he'd requested about the council and portaled to the docks of the undersea city.

His first stop was the Privateer Pub since it was fairly near his arrival point. He'd been told he could leave stuff with the bartender, so he gave the burly man the envelope and a tip. "Keep it safe until my friends come for it." He cut his gaze to the back of the room and the other man nodded.

Thereafter, he began the long walk from the less affluent parts of town—but still fairly moneyed—to the ring of noble houses. Halfway there, his attention was caught by the sunlight flashing off metallic scales and Fyre touched down beside him. He greeted him and held up the envelope he'd brought.

"So, another challenge," the Draksa said.

"I presume so. I'm not sure who from but I found it on Kendra's door." He didn't bother to try to hide his anger. To threaten him was one thing but now that he lived with the detective, a danger to one was more or less a danger to both. "My door, that is."

Frye nodded. "You made a good choice. Her, not so much."

He laughed. "Ah, it's always nice to be back in the warm embrace of your true friends."

The Draksa echoed his amusement and they walked the rest of the way to the house together. When they arrived, Invel opened the door and let them in. "Are you the butler now?" Tanyith asked.

The Dark Elf drew himself up haughtily. "I most certainly am not, Master Tanyith. I am the second butler after Jenkins."

The disembodied voice laughed at the comment and added, "Well, I do have a certain lack of corporeality for things like doors. Perhaps this could be a beneficial arrangement."

Cali came down the stairs and looked happy. "What has you so cheerful?" he asked.

"Oh, nothing big," she replied airily. "I only found the last piece of the sword."

His mouth dropped in surprise and she shared the story with him. When she finished, he couldn't stop grinning. "So, we're most of the way there."

"Yep." She tilted her head to the side. "Did you stop by for a reason? Not that you're not always welcome."

"Oh, yeah. This." He handed her the envelope.

She opened it and nodded. "We're on for the Atlanteans and they say it's the last battle. Apparently, they've reached the same place I'm at with the Malniets."

"When?"

"A week."

"I guess it's time to start training."

"Soon." She grinned. "First, though, I have a matriarch to apologize to and a sword to have repaired."

CHAPTER TWENTY-SIX

Cali hadn't expected another dinner invitation from Wymarc Jehenel after the post-meal activities of the last one and had assumed he'd be too smart to be seen with her until after the current unpleasantness was over. When it arrived in the hands of one of the younger members of his family, she grinned at the smiley face someone had drawn on the missive. She looked sternly at the girl, who must have been all of eleven, and asked, "Did you do this?"

She nodded with a tentative smile. "Yes, Matriarch Leblanc."

"Very well done." She nodded. "Tell the patriarch I'm happy to have a meal with him but I will choose the restaurant." The messenger bounded off happily, and she spent the rest of her day alternately napping and communing with the memories of her parents. It was a melancholy experience all around, and by the time the moment arrived to dress for dinner, she looked forward to the distraction.

Her interest didn't lie in fancy, though, so she dragged jeans and a t-shirt on with boots and her reinforced leather jacket that Nylotte had given her. She put the metal vials containing her energy and health potions into an inside pocket because the part of her life when she felt comfortable being without them in public was now very firmly in the past.

The sound of her guest being admitted to the house reached her, and she descended from her dressing room with Fyre at her heels. She'd made a promise not to leave him behind and that included dinners, dates, or whatever this was. While he wouldn't join them in the restaurant, he'd keep an eye on things from close by and she'd be sure to bring him takeout.

She grinned and gave Wymarc a hug. "You're a glutton for punishment, huh?" He was dressed in an informal suit in navy over a heavy t-shirt, with polished brown shoes. Somehow, he managed to look both casual and elegant in a way she had never once accomplished.

He chuckled. "I guess so. I thought maybe you could use a stress reliever, given all that's going on."

Cali nodded. "Let's hope that's how it turns out, huh?" She didn't comment on the flicker of worry that crossed his features. "Allow me to whisk you away." She summoned a portal that revealed an abandoned alley on the far side and he made a face.

"That does not look like a trendy dining spot."

She laughed. "Go. You too, Fyre." They complied and she followed them through. Their destination was around the corner, and she led Wymarc to it while the Draksa leapt skyward, probably to take a watchful position on the roof like some kind of gargoyle.

Maybe I should get some for the house, ones that look exactly like him. He'd be so annoyed. She made a mental note to look into it at her first opportunity.

The Rum House was a Caribbean restaurant with great food and a casual atmosphere. All the furnishings were wood and the tables were filled with happy couples and groups. The walls held metal signs and lacquered fish of unusual size. She led him in, claimed a seat at the bar, and patted the one beside her. He slid onto it and a bartender approached immediately. She ordered a Coke and he did the same. For some reason, she enjoyed sitting at bars—probably because of all the time she'd spent doing so across from Zeb—even though she didn't drink much alcohol at the moment.

"What's good?" he asked.

Cali shook her head. "Don't worry your pretty little mind about it. I'll take care of this." When the bartender returned, she ordered one of each of the seventeen unique taco options on the menu. She grinned at Wymarc's shocked expression. "They're not all for us. We'll eat the ones that look most interesting and have the rest packed to go. Emalia loves this restaurant and I'm sure Fyre will enjoy whatever's left when she's done."

"Okay, it makes sense. Have you been here much?"

She shook her head. "It's a little out of my price range, usually. But tonight, I felt like splurging."

"Is there a particular reason?" he asked,

While she liked the patriarch of House Jehenel, she didn't trust him. With a shrug, she replied, "Things are looking up, that's all."

"I assumed you'd take me to the bar where you work."

"I considered it but then I'd have to hear about it from

Zeb every single time I went to work." She imitated his low voice. "What's up with that boy from New Atlantis? Are you going to get married soon?"

They both laughed and talked about random subjects until the food arrived. She chose brisket, pulled pork, and fried fish for her three tacos, and he selected duck, chicken, and cauliflower for his.

"So, what do you see for the future of House Jehenel?" she asked.

Wymarc finished chewing, swallowed, and dabbed sauce from his lips with his napkin. "Oh, you know—the usual. Try to increase our wealth, try to increase the size of the family, and try not to be killed by an upstart house with an unexpected vendetta."

Cali shook her head. "If you haven't done anything to earn one, I can't see why that would be a concern for you. Unlike, say, Malniet."

"You never know what kind of secrets might be buried in the past. It could be that an ancestor did someone wrong and they're watching for an opportunity. It's not worth being paranoid about but a smart person wouldn't discount it, either."

"Fair enough." She sighed. "I hope that once this is all over, the Leblanc House can have the same priorities. It would be nice to think there's a normal life of some kind waiting at the end of this long-ass tunnel."

He laughed. "Very poetic."

"No question. Seriously, though, I could do without more drama for a while, I won't lie."

"You could simply step away."

"I can't. Not until Atreo is free and can make that decision with me. But in any case, leaving behind all my parents worked so hard for isn't in the cards."

"I'm glad to hear that. It's always good to have more allies."

She tilted her head to regard him curiously and a little challengingly. "Is that what we are?"

"At least that, I hope." He shrugged. "Ideally, also friends. If not now, then eventually. I'm much less annoying over time."

Cali nodded absently and stared out the window. The foot and vehicle traffic had been fairly consistent while they'd been in the restaurant but suddenly, the pattern had changed and no one was visible.

"*Fyre, what's going on?*" she sent.

His reply was full of concern. "*I can't tell but definitely something. There are no cars coming down the street, and people are moving away from this block like they're worried.*"

"*Magic?*"

"*Who knows?*"

She called the bartender and threw a few bills on the counter. "Bag this, will you? I need to step outside and check something but I'll be right back." She rose and strode to the exit and her companion followed hastily. "You don't have to come," she said.

"Allies, remember? What's going on?"

"I'm not sure yet but Fyre says something definitely is." She stepped out the door and looked in both directions. The block was devoid of other people and the only cars present were those parked on either side. "This is bad. Fyre, get down here. We're leaving."

"What about the tacos?" Wymarc asked.

"Forget them." She circled her arms to create a portal and wasn't completely surprised when it failed to form. "Damn it. Someone's blocking me." He tried as well as Fyre landed beside them.

His failed too. "You were right. This is bad."

She turned to face the patriarch. "Is it you this time too?"

He gaped in shock. "What?"

Cali shook her head. "Cut the act. I know you were behind the last ambush and I know you were working for the Empress. In fact, I also know she told you to put the moves on me so that I'd be emotionally compromised when you betrayed me. So I'll ask again, is this you?" Emalia's listening device had given her all kinds of information about Shenni's efforts to undermine her. She'd been a little hurt but was well aware that the games in Atlantis were never-ending and she needed all the allies she could get.

"No. Absolutely not. Yes, the first one was me, and yes, the Empress told me to deepen our relationship. But I'd decided not to. I didn't intend to contact you again until you reached out. At first, I thought you were merely another noble playing the game. When I finally learned that you weren't, I couldn't be a part of any actions against you. So, no, it's not me."

She sighed and looked past him toward the end of the block. "That's too bad. That means those scary looking people probably intend to kill us for real."

CHAPTER TWENTY-SEVEN

While the group of people she'd seen approached them, Cali walked slowly into the middle of the traffic-free street. The new arrivals had spaced themselves like bowling pins and carried a palpable menace that increased with each step. Unlike the mostly pretend ambush Wymarc had set up—and she wasn't convinced that the mercenaries hadn't planned a double-cross in that situation to eliminate her for real—no sense of restraint was present there.

These people had come to kill her and by accident or design, the patriarch of House Jehenel. *"I see ten,"* she sent to Fyre.

"Agreed. Although they look smart enough to have some in reserve."

She motioned for her dinner companion to stay where he was on the sidewalk so one attack couldn't easily target them both and asked the Draksa, *"Do you think you can lock the back rank down before they realize you're there?"*

"Probably. And if not, I'll distract whoever isn't hit."

"Okay. That's Plan A."

A flicker of amusement registered from him, mostly hidden by the overwhelming concern they exchanged through the channel. *"What's Plan B?"*

"Improvisation." She shook her head and raised her voice to shout across the ten feet or so that remained between her and the enemy. "That's far enough unless you want me to kick this fight off for you. I presume since you haven't attacked already that you wish to inflict some kind of clever speech on me."

Nothing obvious connected the newcomers—no uniforms, no identification patches, and not even a common body type. They weren't mercenaries, she was sure of that. The leader was a tall, thin man who looked like he spent far more time pursuing mental activities than physical ones.

"Nothing clever," he called in response. "I merely felt the need to offer the proper respect to the head of a noble house." He turned his head to Wymarc. "Patriarch Jehenel, this matter doesn't concern you. If you walk away now, you will live."

That banishes any doubt that they're from New Atlantis. And since they don't want to tick Jehenel off, they're either Malniets, their allies, or Styrris' hirelings.

"Gloves off, buddy," she sent. His mental reply was an aggressive growl, the kind that would make any intelligent person who heard it run for safety.

Wymarc gave the man a slight nod. "And here is my counteroffer. If you all walk away, you and whoever sent you will remain untouched by Jehenel. But if you don't, my house will ensure that every last one of you is tracked down, interrogated, and left to spend the rest of your miserable life missing important body parts."

Damn. He sounded serious about the threat and she honestly had no idea if he or his family was capable of making good on it. The enemy clearly didn't think so or perhaps didn't care.

"What will be, will be," the thin man replied, jerked his hands up, and unleashed a cone of fire at her ally.

Her instinct was to protect him, but she knew that was exactly what they'd expect. *I need to get close so they can't all blast me.* She charged the leader and summoned a full body shield to defend her advance. Her hastily crafted barrier activated barely in time and took the impact of fire, lightning, and shadow. In her peripheral vision, Wymarc withstood the attack on him behind his wall of force.

Fyre rippled into visibility as he dove at the back rank and discharged his frost breath across them in a line. Three were caught fully and transformed into statues locked in ice, while the one who ran forward fell with his feet trapped. The Draksa screeched and several of the enemies cringed and stared at him.

His actions took the attention off her. Cali dropped her shield and used a sweeping wave of force at ankle height to hurl two of the attackers, a man and a woman, off their feet. A little voice inside her brain criticized her for not aiming the blow at throat level, but the adventure with the agents had only reinforced her desire to be nonlethal as often as she could. The numbers made the likelihood that everyone would survive the fight low, though.

And if it has to be someone, it won't be us. She channeled all her momentum into a knee strike and hopped at the last minute to target the thin man's solar plexus. He crumpled with an explosive exhale, and she grinned momentarily at the panic on his face. *Serves you right, jerk.*

She paid for her switch to offense when a force bolt drove into the side of her chest and thrust her off balance. Instinctively, she dove in the direction in which she stumbled and shoulder-rolled on the pavement to avoid the follow-up attack, a burst of flame that detonated behind her.

Damn it. Get close and stay close, stupid. She rose as her sticks flowed into her hands and used one to launch a fireball into the air that arced toward the center of the group.

The purpose of the attack was distraction and confusion, and it did its job well. Those enemies who were still mobile scattered in all directions. The man with his feet locked in ice had the presence of mind to throw a ball of fire to intercept hers. When the two met, they shattered into countless falling stars of flame.

She dodged those closest to her and trusted that her allies did the same. Belatedly, she also hoped the nearby buildings wouldn't catch alight but couldn't spare the time to check. She had found her way into the middle of the remaining four assailants and hammered her sticks into whatever body parts were available while she dodged their flailed attacks.

Fyre dove past her, his claws outstretched, and clutched one of them. He flew with the man toward a cafe across the street and flung him into the wall on the second story between two windows that might have allowed him to rejoin the battle. The stone surface he impacted with wasn't as accommodating, and neither was the sidewalk at the end of his fall.

Wymarc's shouted, "Duck," made her fall reflexively to the side and roll and a bolt of lightning surged into the person she'd faced. When she stood, she discovered that the man whose feet had been trapped had freed himself and melted his comrades enough out of their cocoons that they could take care of the rest. The part of her mind in charge of monitoring battle strategy revised the number of active opponents from five to eight again.

Damn it. Right. Gloves off.

Cali lashed out with her sticks at those closest to her. Where before, she'd aimed at elbows and knees, she now targeted heads and necks. In a flurry of strikes, she eliminated two of her adversaries, and a quick breeze followed by a scream that cut off suddenly told her Fyre had removed another from the fight.

Back to five. She spun and raised her sticks in an X to block a cone of fire as she channeled magic through them to reinforce the weapons' defensive ability. She also drew in some of the incoming power and used it to replenish her own as Nylotte had taught her.

Wymarc blasted the woman who attacked her with a jolt of force magic that hurled the enemy through the window to the Rum House, where the customers had already turned the tables on their sides to create cover to shelter behind.

At least she wasn't on fire. That's something, right? A blazing pain seared through her skull and suddenly, she was on the ground with no memory of how she'd gotten there. "*Roll,*" Fyre screamed in her mind, and she complied but almost lost consciousness when agony ripped through her, starting from her head and radiating into her body. She raised a hand reflexively, and it came back bloody.

She heard a noise and realized the Draksa was speaking to her telepathically. He repeated one word over and over, and it took her a moment to identify it and another to realize what it meant. Instinct took control and she yanked out the metal vial with her healing potion and tore the cap off.

As she lifted it to her lips, the thin man she'd thought she'd eliminated from the fight stepped into view and grinned at her. His face looked pale and skeletal, his smile that of a skull. His foot intercepted the container on its way to her mouth and kicked it out of her hand, and her arm fell aside. Her eyelids fluttered, and she fought to maintain consciousness as he shook his head.

"Pathetic. House Malniet bids you farewell, Matriarch."

CHAPTER TWENTY-EIGHT

The man who loomed over her raised his hand and flames gathered in it. Cali was sure she was about to die when a force blast pounded into his face, snapped his bones, and catapulted him away. Her ally—no, friend, after this—knelt behind her and tipped a healing potion to her lips. Fyre screamed and swooped as she coughed on the liquid and she knew he was protecting them both. Finally, she swallowed enough that she could drink properly and drained the vial.

Wymarc helped her to stand and she fumbled in her pocket for the other flask. She popped the top, drank half of it, and offered the rest of the energy potion to him. He nodded and drained it. She stretched her hands forward and her sticks flew into them from different directions. They landed with a solidly reassuring smack into her palms. Her ally darted to her right, intercepted an incoming attack, and countered it.

She turned in search of an adversary and found one a few feet away who streaked lightning blasts at Fyre. She stepped forward, drew her right arm back, and drove her stick into the base of his skull with all the anger and fury she held within her. He collapsed onto his face without making a sound.

Her expression grim but satisfied, she nodded and sought her next target. Only three still stood and she realized the Draksa must have dealt with several while she was down. *"Thanks, buddy,"* she sent.

His mental reply was full of relief. *"Don't you ever do that to me again."*

Despite the situation, she laughed. *"So, it's all about you, is it?"*

Amusement colored the anger and concern that comprised most of his emotions. *"Always."*

She threw her left stick at a woman who was summoning a fireball, and her opponent flinched and lost the spell. She punched with the other weapon to deliver a fist of force into the woman's solar plexus and her adversary backpedaled in shock and pain. Cali added power to her muscles and hurled her remaining stick in a tumbling line at her adversary's forehead. The attack effectively disabled the last of their enemies. She turned in a circle and grinned at Wymarc.

"Well, that wasn't so bad."

He shook his head. "It's not over yet. Turn around."

Fyre was filling her in over their mental connection before she saw the reinforcements with her own eyes. Another four had appeared, harder-looking than their previous opponents. They'd sent the weaker ones in first, not trusting the element of surprise, and instead, hoped to wear them down. It had almost worked.

If Wymarc hadn't stayed, it would have. She retrieved her sticks magically and adopted a fighting stance with her allies on either side of her. "So, you're all Malniets, aren't you?" she called.

The man on the far right grinned. "Maybe, maybe not. It won't matter in the end."

"Did you hear what I told your friends? It still stands," Wymarc stated coldly.

The woman at the other end of the enemy line shrugged. "You'll have to survive to make that happen and that's not in the cards for you, I'm afraid. You should have left when you had the chance, Jehenel."

The man beside her scoffed. "And once your house falls, I'm sure we'll find someone far more useful to replace you."

Cali's ability to cope with the nonsense suddenly evaporated. She growled with quiet fury. "The two in the middle are mine. Fyre, the woman is yours. Wymarc, deal with the first idiot." She let her left stick flow into a bracelet again, summoned a full body shield, and bulldozed forward behind it. The Draksa flew past on her left and dipped and dodged through the gouts of fire two of the enemies directed at him. Her other ally looped to the right to force the one on that side to engage him or risk being flanked.

She lost sight of her teammates as her focus narrowed to the two opponents in front of her. Both were strongly built men and possessed faces that conveyed fighting experience in scars, lines, and intensity. They separated enough to avoid presenting a single target and battered her defenses with every type of magic they had in search of a way through as she closed. By the time she reached them, she'd come to the conclusion that while she might be stronger than either of them individually, they had more power together than she did. *Okay, so I'll have to be smart about it.*

When she leaned out from behind her shield and blasted one with force, he deflected it easily. Her attempted attack on the other accomplished the same result. She growled and shrank her shield to a typical buckler size, threw lightning at the one on her left, and willed it to strike him and link to the other one like a chain. He caught it on his shield, backed away a few steps, and responded with fire that she deflected with her protective barrier. She fell away from him and to the side and rolled to avoid his comrade's shadow blast. Using her momentum, she found her feet in the perfect position to deliver a powerful side-kick to the man's ribs. He managed to lower an elbow to diminish the intensity of the strike and countered with his own, and his longer leg caught her as she retreated.

Cali twisted awkwardly and let herself fall again. When she rolled up, lightning crackled around her body. They both blasted her with force but she poured energy into her magic and it acted as a shield. For the first time, she understood why Nylotte had wanted to teach her to drain others' attacks. Maintaining the intensity of the flow that circled her body made her feel like the effort was draining her. She maintained the shield and willed part of the energy to flow into her hands and spill onto the ground to form whips.

Her enemies tried each of their forms of magic again—fire, force, shadow, ice, and lightning—in an attempt to pierce her defense. She snapped the line of electricity at the man on her right and twined it around his neck. He raised his hands to grasp it, and his power began to flow along the channel that connected them. She frowned, focused, and directed more of her magic down the rope to hold him in check.

The other one had tried to circle, but she lashed the left-hand whip at him before he moved out of range. He called a shield, but she twirled the weapon in the air, evaded the block, and wound her line around his arm. He immediately sent offensive magic down the channel and she blocked it. She felt no pain, only weakness from maintaining her magic.

Their contorted expressions told her that wasn't true for them, and she increased her efforts and pressed harder. They endured and pushed back where they could, apparently having realized the same thing she did. Eventually, she would weaken, and one or both of them would be free to kill her.

She hoped it wouldn't happen until Fyre or Wymarc was ready to help her, but she was so deep in her head that she had no idea what transpired in the larger battle. When she let her senses expand, she detected the interplay of magic from her right, which signified that the Jehenel patriarch was still engaged. She felt Fyre swoop and dart above and sent, *"We need to finish this. Can you hit my targets?"*

"I'll try," he replied but as soon as he altered direction toward them, he cursed in her mind. *"No. If I do, the woman will attack you. I have to keep her running."*

Cali gritted her teeth and pushed more magic at her enemies. She tried to layer the technique Nylotte had taught her to steal some of their power over and above what she was already doing but felt her control of the lightning waver and stopped instantly. She shouted the activation word for her shield charm and it sprang into life, only to immediately fizzle under the barrage from her foes. Their eyes were squeezed closed so her other magical pendant couldn't help.

"Damn it. I'm out of ideas, buddy, and I don't think I can hold these two much longer."

She felt a wave of decision from the Draksa and turned to locate him. He flashed into her line of sight and dove directly into the cone of fire his opponent streaked at him. He waggled from side to side as he approached, but she kept the magic targeted on his body. Cali sensed his pain and his determination and winced when his scales began to scorch. The damage was taking a toll and forced his charge to slow, but the final result was never in doubt. His enemy realized his goal at the last possible moment and threw a shield up to take the impact, but he plowed through it and crushed her into the asphalt, then tumbled and slid until his momentum ended.

"Fyre," she screamed, both out loud and in her mind, and sent another surge down her lines, desperate to break free and check on the Draksa. Her opponents resisted, and tears seeped from her eyes. His consciousness flickered into a dim awareness. *"Get up, buddy,"* she told him. *"Come on. You can do it."*

His dark telepathic chuckle was filled with pain. *"Legs and wings broken. Will take too long to repair. But I can do this."* She sensed it when he summoned his strength and it flowed into her through their mental connection and filled her with power. Rather than hold it, she simply opened a channel from the magical creature to her lightning lines. Her opponents screamed and writhed as the magic shattered their defenses, washed over them, and fell away. In that moment, she couldn't bring herself to care if they were alive or dead.

Cali turned and wrapped the remaining attacker with both lines at the same time and sent a surge through to disable him fast and hard. This one was better controlled and she cut the flow off as soon as he was incapacitated. Satisfied that he would offer no further attacks, she ran to Fyre, knelt beside him, and put her ear on his side to be sure he still breathed and that his heart still beat.

He twitched and muttered, "Ow. Stop it. Broken. Are you stupid?"

Tears of relief streamed down her face as she shouted for Wymarc to portal out and get help. She wound her arms carefully around her partner, put her head on the pavement beside his, and sent every ounce of love she could muster across the enduring connection between them.

CHAPTER TWENTY-NINE

Styrris Malniet was in a rage and privately, Shenni found it deeply amusing. She kept her face serious and nodded while he ranted about the Leblanc girl, the Leblanc family, and any number of other topics. In the corner, Matriarch Cormier huddled quietly and looked decidedly sick.

I'm not sure what or who compelled her to agree to this marriage, but it's starting to look like her best outcome is the fall of Malniet—or at least the demise of its patriarch.

He segued into the need for her to provide him with additional resources and she raised a hand. Instantly, he stopped speaking and apparently retained some mental presence in spite of his fury. "Our arrangement is clear, Styrris. You have a task to accomplish and have committed to do so. Don't come crying to me because it's harder than you expected."

The man—clearly accustomed to using his authority as a bludgeon—scowled at her. "I was under the impression that we were partners in this."

She shook her head. "Then your impression was incorrect. You are one of my subjects and while you and your house have unique things to offer, that does not make you my equal. You would be wise to remember that."

His eyes took on a sleepy look, and she could almost hear him mentally committing to her defeat after he had eradicated the Leblancs. *You're welcome to try, old man.*

"What do you, in your infinite wisdom, suggest I should do, Empress?" he asked after a moment.

The Empress shrugged. "Your ambush failed and clearly, you underestimated the girl. It seems like you would be wise to accept her offer of an early resolution." He gaped and she laughed. "Yes, Styrris, I've heard about it. I dare say everyone has." She looked at the woman who cringed in the corner. "Have you?"

"Yes, Empress," the matriarch replied reluctantly. "I have."

Shenni raised a hand. "See? It's public knowledge now. And given the stunning failure of your family to deal with her when you had the element of surprise, I think you should perhaps try a different tactic."

He folded his arms and glared at her. "Such as?"

"Call in any favors you are owed to secure the best fighters you can find. Limit the final battle to that number. In the meantime, try to remove her allies by whatever means necessary."

"And will you assist with this?"

She smiled. "My Champion is already working on that, although she might not realize it."

Usha struck, parried, and evaded invisible enemies in the darkened gymnasium. The school was closed for the weekend, which permitted her more practice time in the space than usual. She had funneled some of the gang's money to the neighborhood since the day she'd taken over.

This area was home to more Atlantean immigrants than any other part of the city. They had come for new lives and had stayed separate from her organization, which was fine with her. All of them were normal folks from the kinds of places where she grew up, rather than from under the dome. The only thing she asked in return was to use the school gym when the kids didn't, which meant evenings on most weekdays and now that she was training more intensively, weekends as well.

With each action, she visualized a different enemy. Before, it had been Grisham and the members of his gang and occasionally, well-remembered opponents from the tournament that had made her Champion. But today, she saw only two people.

Mostly, she battled Leblanc, who wielded her reforged house sword. The Atlantean leader couldn't shatter it as she'd done before because only one of the magically enchanted weapons could destroy another and her blade was not magical in the least. It was sharp, effective, and as familiar as her own hands but mundane. As a result, the fights in her mind were drawn-out affairs, full of counters, kicks, and every other technique she knew to win an advantage over an opponent. She wondered if the fact that even her own brain wouldn't provide her with a victory should concern her.

The other person she saw at the end of her blade was

one she'd never anticipated—Empress Shenni, her face locked in the look of displeasure she'd worn while she banished her loyal Champion from New Atlantis. She found she couldn't strike the woman and could only defend against the heirloom sword of House Rivette as it sought her life. Finally, dripping with sweat and filled with anger that had no focus, she quit swinging and dropped to the floor. Her mind was a whirl of uncontrolled thoughts, but she constantly returned to the same one.

First, Leblanc. Then, I'll know what to do next.

At that same moment, Danna and Ozahl sat on the couch in their living room, shared a bottle of Merlot, and imagined what their future in New Atlantis would be like. They'd heard about the fight in the Garden District and had agreed it was an unsophisticated move.

"If anything will get to her before you do," the mage said, "it'll be a knife in the dark, not a brawl on the street."

She nodded. "Especially after that. Now, she'll be on her guard against everything. Even if we wanted to eliminate her ahead of time, the idiot Malniets have ruined any chance of it."

He grinned. "Well, love, I guess it's good you decided to play fair, then, isn't it?"

"Yes, though 'fair' might be a strong word, all things considered." She chuckled.

"Oh, really?" He turned on the couch to face her fully. "What are you up to, Danna darling?"

She laughed and pursed her lips in an air kiss. "Only

time will tell, my love. I never will."

In his mansion after meeting the infernal woman who currently occupied the throne, Styrris was no less angry than he had been at any other time that day. His best people—the most accomplished fighters outside the main Malniet bloodline—had failed. *Sure, they almost succeeded, or so they said.* He wondered how hard they'd tried. Loyalty was increasingly difficult to come by.

He considered whether it would be worth simply giving the Leblanc girl what she wanted. The plan to dispossess that family had met with failure, and he'd set his sights on Cormier instead. He was sure everyone assumed his future bride would outlast him. Unfortunately for her, that would not be the case. Before he left this world, he would see at least one more house led by his relatives.

If he played the situation with Leblanc right, it could be two. Part of him knew it was greedy and the rest of him didn't care. When the days behind outnumbered the days ahead, one grew bold.

No, I won't give the girl what she wants. I'll do as the Empress suggests. Accept the challenge and find the best fighters available. He smiled as a new thought occurred to him. *And I'll try to have Matriarch Leblanc killed before, again as Shenni suggests. If the attempt fails, it shouldn't be hard to make sure the evidence points to the palace rather than me.*

He sank into his chair, called for a bottle of wine, and stared into the flickering flames. *Oh, yes, this will work out nicely. Leblanc falls, or the Empress falls. Either way, I win.*

CHAPTER THIRTY

Zeb smiled a welcome at Tanyith and Kendra when they entered the bar. They had both let their hair grow since he'd first met them, which he saw as a sign of their shared contentment. In the same way that old couples grew to resemble one another, they had begun a journey down that path. His was no longer in the ludicrous pompadour, either, but had been slicked back in a more dignified style.

"It's good to see you," he said and retrieved two glasses.

They sat as he pulled a drink for each of them from his homebrew cask, which was a mead today but a perilously strong one. Even he had to watch his intake, and that said it all.

"How are you?" Kendra asked.

He shrugged and handed them the drinks, then drew a short one for himself. "Good, good. Things have been mostly quiet, although I think Janice is a little tired from working such long days."

Their heads turned to find the server, who did a great

job taking care of the customers, as always. She wasn't as entertaining as Cali, though, and the tavern was less exuberant because of it.

Tanyith must have thought the same because he asked, "Will Cali come back to work soon?"

The dwarf nodded. "She'll take on a few days, she said. That'll be good and give everyone else a break."

"Except the customers," Kendra quipped, and they all laughed.

Zeb stroked his beard thoughtfully. "Hey, Tanyith, you're not all that busy lately, right?"

The man chuckled and it had a tinge of embarrassment to it. "I'd say that's accurate. Mainly, I wait for my girl-friend to get home." The couple exchanged a grin. "I don't lack money at the moment but I'll admit I'm a little bored. Why do you ask?"

"I thought maybe you could spend a few days a week here in the afternoons to help out. You're a natural with people and you'd be able to pick it up fast. After a while, I might even be willing to teach you how to brew."

Tanyith took a sip as he considered the offer. When he could, Zeb tried to match his requirements with others' needs. It was why he'd hired Cali, despite her lack of experience, when she'd needed something to focus her energy on. He'd done the same for Janice when her freelance art career hadn't been enough to make ends meet while her husband decided what he wanted to do with his professional life. It was apparent that the former prisoner wasn't on a particular path other than supporting Cali and having a routine to keep him steady certainly wouldn't hurt.

Finally, the man nodded. "I'd love that. When do I start?"

He grinned. "Tomorrow at nine in the morning. You get to help me with the stew."

"Perfect." His body language sent the same message, which told him he'd made the right choice yet again.

His internal voice intruded. "*Once you have a group of people who are able to take over for you, maybe you can get back to what you're really good at.*" Involuntarily, he looked at the battle-ax that he'd returned to her place above the bar. *No. That part of my life is in the past.*

Laughter echoed inside. "*Sure it is. Keep telling yourself that.*"

For the first time, Cali was able to visit Stonesreach without having to walk the whole way from the tunnel. Nylotte had met her at the Bulldog in New Orleans and portaled her to the Kemana. They talked quietly as they walked to Alessand's shop, but the Dark Elf clearly understood that her mind couldn't focus on any thoughts other than the sword.

Even Fyre, who trotted at her side, didn't try to talk to her. It felt like the end of a long journey, although she knew it wasn't. At best, it was the middle. *Okay, maybe two-thirds of the way.* But she still had significant challenges to deal with.

The master craftsman waited for them in his front room and led them to the back. A large table stood in the center made of stone with carvings that filled every surface, runes and letters in yet another alphabet she didn't recognize. On it lay the pieces of the sword she'd already delivered, correctly arranged. She shrugged her backpack off, removed the last two shards, and handed them to him.

He set them in place and nudged all the fragments together so it went from the appearance of an assemblage of separate items to looking like a single weapon with many cracks in it. He nodded. "Okay. The moment of truth. Please step back."

They complied, and a shimmering force shield spread in a circle from the surface beneath the shards. Only then did she notice the carvings on the floor, which matched some of those on the table. Alessand closed his eyes and extended his hands toward the sword.

A piece rose into the air, followed shortly by another. As the second neared the first, the edges appeared to turn to liquid and flow together, and after a flash of brilliance, they were one. The process repeated as he reconstructed the blade one section at a time until only the hilt was left.

Nylotte leaned closer to her and whispered, "Don't be alarmed, but this is the pivotal moment, the hardest part."

Concern sparked in her mind. "How come?"

The Drow shrugged. "I have no idea. That's what he said."

Cali sighed, exasperated. "Why are you telling me this when I can't do anything about it?"

The woman responded with a wicked smile. "Because it's fun to watch you worry."

Her snarled response was preempted by a growing incandescence that covered the two remaining pieces on the table. She had to close her eyes against the glow and when she opened them, the sword master stood with his hand extended as the weapon, now fully repaired, descended into it.

The shield fell and he rested the blade across his forearm and turned to present it to her. "I believe this belongs to you, Matriarch Leblanc."

She grasped the hilt and a surge of emotion flowed through her at the knowledge that she'd reclaimed a piece of her parents' history and solved half the puzzle of her brother's release. It took a long moment before she managed to force the words out. "Thank you."

He nodded. "You're welcome."

"What will you do now?" Nylotte asked.

Cali stared at the tip of the sword, which looked sharp enough to cut through reality itself. A certainty of purpose replaced her emotional response to receiving the weapon. When she spoke, it felt like making a vow. "I'll learn as much as possible about how to fight with a sword so that I can stick this into Styrris Malniet and twist it until he tells me how to free Atreo."

The story doesn't end here. Join us for the exciting conclusion to the series in *The Last Dance!*

If you enjoyed this book, you may also enjoy the first series from T.R. Cameron, also set in the Oriceran Universe. The Federal Agents of Magic series begins with Magic Ops and it's available now at Amazon and through Kindle Unlimited.

FBI Agent Diana Sheen is an agent with a secret…

…She carries a badge and a troll, along with a little magic.

But her Most Wanted List is going to take a little extra effort.

She'll have to embrace her powers and up her game to take down new threats,

Not to mention deal with the troll that's adopted her.

All signs point to a serious threat lurking just beyond sight, pulling the strings to put the forces of good in harm's way.

Magic or mundane, you break the law, and Diana's gonna find you, tag you and bring you in. Watch out magical baddies, this agent can level the playing field.

It's all in a day's work for the newest Federal Agent of Magic.

Available now at Amazon and through Kindle Unlimited

Thank you for reading the seventh book in the *Scions of Magic* series! Things are accelerating like a runaway train, and I hope you're excited to see how it ends!

March felt like it lasted about ninety days. I am lucky enough that I can work from home, as can my wife, and my kid is homeschooled, so we're all together. I can't imagine what it's like to be living a "normal" life in this situation. For all of you who are still out and about making the world go 'round, thank you so much for your efforts.

I've been finding mental balance through entertainment; I'm sure many are in the same boat. Rereading books that I love, rewatching shows and movies, seeking comfort in the familiar. We're currently moving onto season 3 of *Justified*, which is perhaps the best-written show on television, ever. Some people might counter with *The Wire* for that particular distinction, and I can respect that, too. In my book, *The Expanse* is up there, too.

I started a new video game, Jedi: Fallen Order. I've been selecting media content lately mainly based on story, and so far this one is really good. I'm a fan of both *Wars* and *Trek*, so for me this fills in a gap between *The Clone Wars* and *A New Hope* nicely.

My kid and I had grand plans for the summer involving travel, amusement parks, and a family wedding. The wedding is postponed, the idea of being around crowds at an amusement park is currently beyond daunting, and since the travel was mostly *for* amusement parks, it looks like a plan B will be required.

I'm hoping the world comes out the other side of the current experience with the realization that what has really made a difference so far, what really matters, is community. The connection to others, however we can do so, is being proven again and again to be a vital part of thriving in the world, physically and emotionally. I think many of us who are "readers" already know that – it's so fundamental to so many of the stories we write and read.

This is a place where we as a group were definitely ahead of the curve, especially those who have read science fiction and fantasy where such ideas are commonly explored from a variety of viewpoints.

Okay, off the soapbox. I hope you are well, and I hope you do all you can to stay well. Many adventures lie ahead.

Until next time, Joys upon joys to you and yours – so may it be.

PS: If you'd like to chat with me, here's the place. I check in daily or more: https://www.facebook.com/AuthorTRCameron. Often I put up interesting and/or silly content there, as well. For more info on my books, and to join my reader's group, please visit www.trcameron.com.

I think we're in week 5 of sheltering in place. It's taken on its own kind of normal, right? As it turns out we are a very adaptable species. Good news. More good news, we are also very creative and giving as well.

There's been an explosion of creativity from the weird to the wow, look what they can do! I've seen an art museum for pet gerbils complete with recreations of famous paintings but with gerbil faces instead. (One of the gerbils was nibbling on a tiny chair. Must not have read the sign that said, 'no touching'.)

Plenty of choreographed dance moves with multi-generations involved. The two grown sons lifting their dad was a particular favorite. But then there's the people who are taking amazing photographs of sunsets right off their back porch, or people showing off their prowess with violins and guitars and banjos. Even better, they're generally playing outside so that their neighbors can enjoy it as well.

Authors are reading their books, museums are showing off their collections, zoos are inviting you inside, musicals are all online and movies that were meant for a theater are available right now on your TV.

Then there's the people, like me, who have dusted off their sewing skills and are busy making masks and headbands with buttons for nurses and neighbors. Or signs to thank grocery store workers and custodians. Or a lot of homemade bread that gets shared around a neighborhood. I'm going to take a whack at gluten-free English muffins this weekend.

My neighborhood has collectively done painted rocks that people leave while on a walk so that their fellow walkers can suddenly come upon a tiny rainbow. We've also left giant words of encouragement in our windows for each other like 'Love' or 'Joy' and posted big paper Easter eggs everywhere for the kids to hunt, and a weekly Zoom happy hour with games. Tonight, there's a virtual dance party.

Other neighborhoods have done drive by birthday parties, so someone knows they weren't forgotten. A small group of us had warm cookies delivered to a neighbor on her birthday. She FaceTimed me biting down on one, a big smile on her face, to let me know it was appreciated. We've also done group runs for vegetable and fruit boxes and getting meat from a local rancher. The list is kind of endless.

So is how much we are all learning to care for and appreciate each other in ways we may not have had time for, or wouldn't have thought necessary in the past. I hope this is one of those things we take with us after this is all over. More adventures to follow

Note: If you find this book years from now when it's all in the rear-view mirror – wasn't that something?

Facebook Here: https://www.
facebook.com/TheKurtherianGambitBooks/